Young

Also from Islandport Press

Billy Boy
by Jean Mary Flahive

My Life in the Maine Woods
by Annette Jackson

Contentment Cove
by Miriam Colwell

Stealing History
by William D. Andrews

Shoutin' into the Fog
by Thomas Hanna

down the road a piece: A Storyteller's Guide to Maine and
A Moose and a Lobster Walk into a Bar
by John McDonald

Windswept, Mary Peters and *Silas Crockett*
by Mary Ellen Chase

Nine Mile Bridge
by Helen Hamlin

Titus Tidewater
by Suzy Verrier

At One: In a Place Called Maine
by Lynn Plourde and Leslie Mansmann

In Maine
by John N. Cole

The Cows Are Out! Two Decades on a Maine Dairy Farm
by Trudy Chambers Price

These and other Maine books are available at:
www.islandportpress.com.

Young
By Miriam Colwell

ISLANDPORT PRESS

ISLANDPORT PRESS • FRENCHBORO • NEW GLOUCESTER

Islandport Press
P.O. Box 10
Yarmouth, Maine 04096
www.islandportpress.com

Copyright ©1955, 2008 by Miriam Colwell
All rights reserved. Printed in U.S.A.

First Islandport Press Edition, May 2008
Young was originally published by
Ballantine Books, Inc. in 1955.
This Islandport Press edition is published by arrangement
with the author.

ISBN: 978-1-934031-16-2
Library of Congress Card Number: 2008921471

Book jacket design by Karen F. Hoots / Hoots Design
Cover image courtesy of iStockphoto / Julie Frame
Book design by Michelle A. Lunt / Islandport Press
Photo page 180 copyright ©2008 by Linda Eastman

*This book is affectionately dedicated
To Whom it may Concern*

Also by Miriam Colwell

Wind off the Water

Day of the Trumpet

Contentment Cove

A few words from
Miriam Colwell

After the publication of my second novel, *The Day of the Trumpet*, in 1947, I worked for the next five or six years on a manuscript set in the 1800s that I called *Pilgrimage*, or sometimes, *Justin*. Month after month, year after year I wrote, revised, sent it off, got it back, and revised some more. Bernice Baumgaten, my patient agent, sent it out many times to publishers though she must have known it should have been strangled at birth. I even made the unfortunate decision to change agents hoping new blood would help. But it didn't. So at long last Justin and I finally ended our *Pilgrimage*.

Ave et vale.

I began thinking of a quite different subject, after being bogged down in the mid-19th century so long. My working title for the new manuscript was *After Midnight*, but it was only after I dropped the third person approach and let Evelyn tell her story that it began to take shape.

In October, 1953, Chenoweth wrote in her journal, "Mimi is started like a rocket on her new book." It was a cold snowy fall and winter, but writing *After Midnight* was sheer pleasure. Many afternoons I would insist that Chenoweth stop whatever she was doing to listen to the day's installment, which always amused and delighted me quite as though I hadn't spent the morning writing it.

In mid-January, after a financial conference, Chenoweth and I regretfully decided to give up plans for a cross-country trip to California and pay bills instead. That noble decision helped our credit standing, but in early February I had what might be called a mini-breakdown in the post office, just at mail time. Our doctor could find no physical cause other than a slight anemia.

While I was recuperating, one of those miracles of friendship happened that usually happen only in fiction. A close friend sent me a check for $3000 with a note: "It's for the trip, rest, change, wherever suits you at this time."

So it came about after all that on March 1, 1954 we left our Prospect Harbor home on a two and a half month drive across the continent. In Tucson, Arizona, we stopped for two weeks while I fiinished typing the manuscript and sent it off to the new agent in New York.

That sorry adventure lasted through the summer and fall, until finally *Almost Midnight* got back to Bernice at Brandt and Brandt and she sold it almost immediately to Ian Ballantine of Ballantine Books in November.

Bernice wrote to me on December 8 of that year, "I am a little disappointed that you're not coming down because it would have been so much easier for you to talk to Stanley Kauffman, Ballantine's wonderful editor, and to Ian himself, about the suggested changes, but Stanley is going to write you fully . . ."

December was not an easy time for me to take leave from the post office, and Stanley certainly wrote fully! His first letter ran to six closely spaced pages. Most of his suggested changes were minor, but a few caused an intense exchange of letters. At the same time my work was heating up with Christmas mail, and I was trying to get the revisions done. They wanted the revised manuscript by January 1.

The skirmishes included a title. Ian and Stanley were united on *The Troublemakers*. I was united that it would never be! Fortunately, Bernice discovered that it was already taken. Then they felt that the poem was too long. In fact, why not skip it entirely? A copy editor, with her own mania, chose to sprinkle semicolons through the manuscript like a heavy spring shower, replacing every comma.

Young was published on February 11, 1955, minus semicolons. The title was theirs.

There was a second printing in December, as well as a British edition by Weidenfeld and Nicholson, although their regular printer refused to do the job on grounds of obscenity!

A small movie offer came along, spurned by my agent, but in 1963 a contract was signed with Seven Arts Productions. Work had begun on a screenplay and casting, when one of the featured actresses was hurt in a car accident, postponing operations, which were fated not to resume. But on the strength of the proposed film, Ballentine published a large new edition.

Thirty years later in 1997, Constance Hunting in Orono, Maine brought out her handsome small Puckerbrush Press edition.

Now to the present moment, and a new Islandport Press *Young*!

Miriam Colwell
Prospect Harbor, Maine
May 2008

Miriam Colwell was born and raised in Prospect Harbor, Maine, where she was postmaster for more than thirty years. She published four popular novels set in Maine: *Wind off the Water* (1945), *Day of the Trumpet* (1947), *Young* (1955), and *Contentment Cove* (2006). For more about Miriam, please read the About the Author section at the end of this novel.

Part I
Morning
page 3

Part II
Afternoon
page 51

Part III
Night
page 87

Part IV
After Midnight
page 153

Part I

Morning

I woke up squinting. The sun shines right into my eyes in the morning. Because of the way my room faces. Every morning for three weeks without a variation it had been the same exact story. Not a cloud in the sky.

My furniture was all bright yellow too, even if the label on the can said Starlite Gold, and that didn't help. I could have pulled down the shades, naturally, but I hate drawn shades. Especially at night. It's like crawling into a hole and pulling the hole in after you.

A nice gloomy old rainstorm that morning might have stayed the hands of fate. Who's to say?

Anyhow, the minute I went staggering downstairs, more dead than alive from all that glaring sunshine and the night I'd had, my mother was at me. Her orders had to be delivered, as if I didn't know.

"Mercy, I'm glad you're up, Evelyn. So you can get started out with these orders. I haven't got a place left to set a thing. Well, dear, Charlie's gone, has he? How did he feel, it being your last night together? In *my* estimation, it will be his making to get away from home and hold down a job. I've no doubt in the world he'll do well if they have the sense to keep him busy. He puts up a fine appearance and he's light on his feet. That's what they need in a summer hotel.

"Now, what do you want for breakfast? Oh my Lord, it doesn't seem as if I could draw a breath till I get all this bread from under foot."

"All *right*, Mother dear," I said. "But first let me barely draw a breath, for Pete's sake. All I want is a doughnut. A *store* doughnut."

Her orders were all over the kitchen: cinnamon buns and oatmeal bread and yeast rolls and raisin muffins and rye loaves and plain loaves and loaves and loaves.

Just the smell made my head ache. Not to mention all the Oh, be joyful sunshine pouring in.

I took my coffee in the other room, and found one old crumpled cigarette in a pack Dad had left for dead on the windowsill. The Christmas cactus needed water and there was a dust mouse curled around the piano leg, but I certainly didn't feel like noticing.

I had problems to consider. Real problems. Evelyn faces life and so on. It was no joke to be my age and suddenly find yourself through school and confronting the big question, What Next?

In the receiving line at graduation when I shook hands with Mr. Becker, he said, "These have been the best years of your life here in this school, Evelyn. The best years of your life."

In a way it was true, and I knew it. But Charlie laughed almost in his face, and all the time he kept shaking hands and passing people along with his big personality-boy act (". . . and this is Miss Urquhart . . ."), Charlie kept hissing in my ear, "Best years of your life, sweet suffering Jesus! In *this* town? I'd hate to think so."

But Mr. Becker was right, even if it was the only thing he ever bothered to say to me except hello.

To tell the truth, I was really weighed down that morning. With those four years at Eastern High behind me and the future looming ahead. What next? That was the big problem.

With Charlie it was different. He was entering the Maritime Academy in the fall to become an officer and a gentleman. Bigger miracles *have* happened. And after four years he would be commanding an engine room or something, making a fortune every month as well as wearing a uniform.

He thought that was all there was to it, being pretty naive even if his mother did subscribe to *The New Yorker*. But I knew better. There'd never be those carefree days again, with nothing but basketball games to agonize about, or who was getting the lead in the Senior play, or whether I could get away with a date while he thought I was at home in bed having cramps.

That was a closed chapter, even if I was the only one who realized it.

But my mother had only one thought that morning, and it was not my future. One thought at a time was her normal speed. But, believe me, the one she had she really rolled around and cuddled. To wit, I should instantly totter forth and deliver the bread. Naturally I intended to, but for a while I couldn't do anything but sit there and brood, with the sun getting hotter and hotter and the cactus droopier. Also on top of everything else was the God-awful smell.

Most of the bread went to summer people. They used to have cooks, but now they just bought my mother's bread and ate out. She was cook for the Ogden's herself in the g.o.d.'s. That was when anybody with money expected to have a few pads stuck under the grocery bill. So it wouldn't bounce. Now, the more money they had the harder they held onto it. Would my mother have made a big stink in Tucker's store because they overcharged her week's grocery bill by twenty cents? She never bothered to add it up. If she had, chances are she wouldn't have said anything, because Tucker is as touchy as a wet hen and might have cut off her credit.

But old lady O. added hers up. I was there. It was a big, sad moment in her day.

Anyway, *one* thing I knew about my future: I had to move on. A lot of people don't realize what it means to grow up in a small town. Of course someone like my mother wouldn't live anywhere else, so she says, but with me, it's strictly murder.

You draw a deep breath or gargle your throat, and every blessed person in town can tell if you used Listerine or S.T. 37. And naturally vice versa. You know if they're constipated, how two bottles of Schlitz affects them, who voted four times for Roosevelt and who buys real butter.

Even if a stranger—raise the flag!—a real live stranger, goes walking by, it's ten minutes before you know that he and his wife are visiting at Forrest Kimball's and that last time they came his fat wife who is afraid of cats got in a row with Forrest who thinks a good deal more of his cats than of his relatives.

Personally, I was ready for something a little more exciting, somewhere where six hundred people meant a crowd at the movies, not the entire population. Even at my tender age I had lapped the saucer dry, believe me.

But that led to the first big hurdle. To go anyplace I had to have money. Quite a lot, because everything had gone into graduation—pictures and invitations and a ball gown, and a weekend trip to Boston for the graduating class. I owed my mother forty-two dollars that she had borrowed from the Credit Union, and on top of that I needed new clothes, most of mine being threadbare.

I borrowed a dress and a suit to wear in Boston from the Domestic Science teacher. She was only four years older and the same size, and in exchange I let her drive Francis around while we were gone.

Francis was my old Dodge. He was about a hundred and ten but he managed to get me to school and deliver the orders, and we were very close.

But she didn't click with the old boy, and the first time they started out she couldn't make the brakes work and ran into the back of Kerr's pickup truck on Main Street. The horn on the wheel didn't toot, as I had carefully explained, but she was the excitable type and forgot all about ringing the bicycle bell.

I guess she and Pappy Kerr had quite a discussion. His truck was only a month old. Anyhow she never drove Francis the rest of the time. He just sat in the yard and had a good rest. I was just as glad, because she wasn't a very good driver.

To add to my troubles, Charlie's being away bell-hopping all summer was a nuisance. Actually I didn't mind his being away, as being tied down cramped my style, but this way he would never be around when I wanted him and just when I didn't, surprise! there he'd be, expecting me to jump for joy.

I wanted another cup of coffee, but my mother was all ready to sputter the minute she remembered what to sputter about, and what I needed more was a time of quiet meditation. I poked around trying to find some more cigarettes, but trust my big-hearted old man not to leave any. Just then the telephone rang so I sneaked out the side door.

Francis was sitting on the slope across the yard because his battery was weak, but my mother, who is usually good for a half-hour on the phone even if it's the business office saying we haven't paid last month's bill, wasn't missing a trick.

"Evelyn!" She made a lovely foghorn when she got excited. "*Where* are you off to? Here's all these orders sitting here right in my way, and Mrs. Ogden's just this minute called about her oatmeal bread."

"I know, I *know*, Ma," I called soothingly. "Don't get so excited, you'll raise your blood pressure again. First, I got to sweep out the back of the car. Then I'm going to go get Susan to help. It's easier with two."

With that settled, Francis and I went limping off down the hill. I dearly loved my mother, but there were times when we got on each other's nerves.

Anyhow, it was a fine idea to get Susan. It would take me forever to load all that in alone. And she *liked* the smell. She could sit in back and die of it if she wanted to.

Susan lived with the Beckers. She was their niece, and had lived with them ever since her parents were in an accident practically before she was born.

As long as I happened to be passing Mr. Becker's barbershop I stopped in to see if he knew where she was. He was sitting in the window smoking, and if you hadn't known, very likely you might have taken him for a statue. Except that once in a while a puff of smoke came from his pipe. Not often, too much exertion. His head was shiny and bald and his nose was enormous, though he wasn't bad when he was young, from a picture Susan showed me.

In the memory of time old man Becker never had a fight with anybody—he couldn't be bothered. He couldn't be bothered to collect money people owed him, or sweep up the dead flies and whiskers, or clean the empty boxes out of the candy showcase. Susan did that, but he hated to have her bother him by coming in. Most of all, I think, he hated customers. They were really a disturbing element. Then he had to get up and mill around in front of his old mirror, with all the dirty shaving mugs and dandruff lotions and bay rum bottles and scissors and crumpled towels and razors and straps and combs and brushes lying around, and cut somebody's hair. Or shave them.

Consequently, with that kind of disposition he didn't take much revenue home to Mrs. Becker. She was a different story altogether. She was slight and sharp-nosed and smart as a cricket, and she insisted on having the house painted and the grass cut and the chicken house repaired and the water pipes replaced when they rusted out, which was fortunate, because he wouldn't have been very bothered with any of those things as long as he had a rocking chair to sit in and something to fill his stomach with three times a day. Maybe he could have managed on less than three times. It must have seemed a bother to have to get up and walk home.

Mrs. Becker was the best cook in town outside of my mother, who was practically as good. Everyone knew it. I used to eat there a lot with Susan, and every time Mrs. Becker put jelly tarts in Susan's lunch at school she always put one in for me too because she knew I liked them so much. She was like that, always doing thoughtful things, but never so you had to think about it. Whenever I ate at their house it was always the same. Mr. Becker would come hurrying in—that is for him it was hurrying, because he had to get right back to the barbershop, to sit in the window and smoke his pipe—anyhow, he'd steam into the pantry to the sink, sozzle some water over his face, blow like a walrus, and come out to the table putting in his lower plate. He never wore his lower plate except at meals, because the first time he tried to smoke with it forty years ago it made him gag.

Probably the pipe was so strong the teeth couldn't stand it. Anyhow, he always clamped them in good, sat down as though he didn't have a minute to spare, and began shoveling. As though it was so much shredded wheat. I remember one partridge stew with dumplings—but I guess I'll never forget any of her meals.

Whenever they were having a boiled dinner with spareribs Susan asked me home with her just as a matter of course. Brother! I could have died right there in front of that platter, carrots and cabbage and parsnips and turnips, beets and onions and naturally potatoes, all flavored but heavenly with those old spareribs, or with corned beef. Even when Mrs. Becker made vegetable soup it was fit for a king. And remember my own mother was no slouch.

But Mr. Becker never knew the difference. He just stowed it away so he could go back and sit in the sun at the shop, with a fly swatter handy. He couldn't be bothered with a screen door, but he kept a fly swatter under his chair, and whenever one lighted on him he'd reach for the swatter and bat it. He used to keep score of how many he got for the day.

One summer Mrs. Becker began to take people in for meals, and that's how she could keep things up. That's how Susan had a bicycle, too, when not many kids had one, except the summer boys. Mrs. Becker thought the world of Susan; she never made her do any of the housework or help with the dishes or anything. She hired someone to come in and do them. Susan was pretty spoiled when you came to think of it, but she was so queer other ways it didn't show too much.

I said, "Hello, Mr. Becker. You know where Susan is?"

He just shook his head and aimed at the spittoon under the window. Probably he had been snoozing. There was a fly buzzing around his head and he had a startled look as though everything was happening at once.

"Guess I'll buy a package of gum," I said, just to make him get up. That was a laugh. I should have known better.

"Go help yourself, Evelyn."

He didn't even turn his head while I went behind the counter and opened the candy case.

Someone was in the back playing pool. I could hear the balls clicking.

I took two packages of gum as long as I was doing the work, and then—there sat all those cartons of cigarettes. It was too much for mere flesh and blood. Plums for the picking. Another carton was nearer (which shall be nameless), but they always smelled to me like tobacco crossed with cow manure, so I reached over for a package of Chesterfields.

Mr. Becker was watching the grain man unload in front of Tucker's General Store across the street, and it occurred to me that Susan liked Kools, so I got a package for her. Her uncle ought to be willing to furnish her with cigarettes once in a while; he didn't do much else for her.

It was providential that I had on Charlie's basketball jacket with nice deep pockets. I slammed the case shut and said, "Package of Juicy Fruit, Mr. Becker." He just grunted. There was a nickel lying there on top of the counter that someone had left for a candy bar. He hadn't bothered putting it in the cash drawer. A person so careless about money is just beyond me.

I carried it over to him for the gum, and he grunted again and put it in his pocket. On the other hand, people say he's got the first cent he ever made, so maybe he's just as well off as if he were a ball of fire, easy come, easy go.

The flies were buzzing and the pool balls clicking. No wonder he couldn't keep awake. I peeked out to see who was amusing themselves, and it was no surprise. Jonas Kerr. Whom I had known since before the flood. In looks Jonas was sort of an attractive cross between Gary Cooper and a grizzly bear. Also he had the whitest teeth anybody ever saw, though he probably never brushed them more than twice a month. "Evelyn!" He gave with a big grin, just as if I didn't know him. "Come out and play a game. What's the matter, you lost your best friend, dear?"

"I'm as ugly as sin this morning, Jonas," I said, "just between us two."

He really was a goat, as everyone had reason to know.

"Well, come tell Papa all about it." He put down his cue and began to pad around the table. The way he walked made you think of a bear too, a big, light-on-his-feet sort of young bear.

"Oh God, I haven't got time." I gave him a little smolder over my shoulder, just for the hell of it—you never knew when you might have a flat tire or something—and then I let the door shut in his face.

Francis was waiting keen as mustard, and we shot off in a cloud of exhaust just as Jonas sailed out onto the steps, his cheeks aglow. Mr. Becker had his fly swatter suspended, uncertain whether to swat or watch what Jonas was up to.

That little encounter cheered me up. I drove into Susan's yard and hopped out, feeling that the day might be bearable after all, if she'd just help me with those darned orders. You could usually count on Susan for something like that, something none of the other kids would be caught dead doing, but ask her to come along on a wienie roast as some guy's date and she'd get that real withdrawn look in her eyes and say she was busy.

She never would talk much about things like that, except that she didn't like so-and-so, whoever it was, and I must say, looking at some of the characters around you couldn't blame her, but after all, as I often tried to tell her, better hop on the merry-go-round. Who knows when it may run out of gas? If she didn't like her date, latch onto someone else's.

In this world if you don't make your own opportunities, who does? But she was funny plenty of ways, even if she was the smartest girl in school. Salutatorian of our class, but she should have been valedictorian. Charlie got that because they always jiggled the marks around so a boy would get it. More appropriate or something.

But for anyone so intelligent, it was hard to believe she could be so dumb. When one of the kids told a dirty story in the hall between classes, she'd laugh and laugh like everybody else, but I knew just by her expression she didn't have any more idea what they were talking about than the water cooler.

The trouble was she had a funny proud streak. Even to me she never would admit she didn't know what French kissing meant, or actually much of anything else referring to the bare old facts of life, which was the favorite topic at school, naturally. Believe me, this kid didn't even know what the situation was when a boy got excited. She was touchy about not knowing, like a cat with a chip on its shoulder, all ready to spit and run.

I guess I knew Susan better than anybody else in school. It was comic our being best friends, because we were certainly two different kettles of fish. Maybe that was why, she was a study to me and vice versa.

When I got there Mrs. Becker was in the living room having a heart-to-heart talk with Mrs. Ogden. That old turnip was the last person I was anxious to see, but they both heard me come in.

"Why, Evelyn!"

Mrs. Becker wasn't very pleased with me as Susan's nursemaid, but she never let it come out on the surface. What she said was to Susan, I guess.

"She went down toward the Lighthouse for a walk. About ten minutes ago. You probably know where she goes better than I do. Won't you come in and sit down?"

"No, thanks. I'll go find her, Mrs. Becker."

"Evelyn?" Mrs. Ogden always sounded as though she had a sore throat and was trying to avoid using it. She was about ten feet tall and had a lot of white hair piled on top of that, and real cold blue eyes. Her husband was a high-society minister, and

Mrs. O. had lots of dough inherited from darning needles. They lived in Cambridge, winters.

When I was little I was sure Mrs. Ogden must be a close relation of God's. It wasn't anything she ever said, as she always smiled and asked about school and so on, but believe me, she made a very strong impression. It wasn't her age, exactly, or because she had money. It was just difference.

The Ogdens had their dinners at Mrs. Becker's all summer, and the old girl really liked Mrs. Becker a lot. In fact, she thought it was dreadful for dear Clara to have to work so hard getting meals for summer people. She should know whereof she spoke, as everyone said the Ogdens ate enough at Clara Becker's at noon to last them the whole day.

Sometimes when I delivered the bread order, her daughter would be there on a visit, and then I would hang around just as long as possible. Odessa was her daughter's name, from the happy circumstance that happened wherever it is, when Mr. and Mrs. Ogden were traveling around the world.

It was very hard for me to imagine Mr. and Mrs. Ogden getting right down to the business, but there was the living proof. Odessa was a painter and a writer and a photographer and whatever else you can think of that's artistic. And her husband was worse, judging from his appearance. Anyhow, she was so full of artisticness that I never thought she had much common sense.

One day just as I got out of the car, Odessa came staggering across the lawn pulling a rotten old piece of tree stump. She was the kind of person you always looked back at, partly because she was so young to have white hair. She wore it straight back in a knot and she had dark eyes and real dark eyebrows, and her clothes were always odd too, long full skirts and long silver earrings and bracelets and lots of rings. Or tight black riding pants that would have made Jonas pop his eye sockets, and a thin white blouse with long sleeves. Nothing you ever saw in Sears and Roebuck.

She always looked queer beside everyone else, but it was a queer you were jealous of, not the queer you laughed at, or maybe I did that too.

The tree stump she had was a treasure, in her opinion, and I had to help her carry it up on the porch. Real careful.

"Moth-a . . ." she kept shrieking. "Isn't it perfectly heavenly! I've got to paint it. Oh, look at the beautiful lichen and the magnificent textures."

Lichen! It was so rotten it had moss starting to grow. For a while I thought she meant she was going to paint it yellow or red or something, but she meant she was going to sit down and paint a *picture* of it.

I guess she had the time if that's what she got a bang out of, but believe me I could think of other things to do. Once in a while when she wasn't around I had a chance to go out through the shed that she used for a studio. It was educational. That girl was a real study. I never could decide whether she was practically a genius or just crazy.

Some of her pictures were as lifelike as anything, like one of an old house, and another one of a man with a couple of days' beard. But then all around the man who hadn't shaved were six or seven doors, some of them wide open with blue sky showing through and some just open a crack. That was all there was to that picture, at least as long as she stayed.

The old house I got pretty fond of; every week I would peek in to see if anything had been changed, until one day—and you can believe this or not—she had a big gray rat going in the front door. There he was, half in and half out, with his snaky old tail down over the step.

It was so lifelike it curdled my blood. I hate rats. Francis coughed all the way home, I hurried him so. Anyhow, that was Odessa. Her husband was supposed to be a famous painter, which was how she came to start in. Mrs. Becker had newspaper clippings about him.

Maybe so. But all I can judge is from a couple of samples the Ogdens have, and brother, if that's what it takes to be famous, let me rest in peace.

One hangs by their hall door and one in the parlor. They never use either room much. The things are real big and I can only describe them as follows: two or three thousand colored blobs, plus some straight lines, plus some crooked ones, plus a few run-over caterpillars. Also a few rockets bursting here and there and some squares to play tic-tac-toe in.

According to Susan, Reverend Ogden calls them Jumble #2 and Jumble #3, which sent him up about nine hundred percent in my esteem. She was sorry the minute she told me that, because of course she likes Odessa's husband. Trust Susan to go for someone full of static.

"Evelyn?" the old turnip said. "I hope you've got my oatmeal bread with you."

"I'm just on my way home for it, Mrs. Ogden," I said, looking her straight in the eye. "My mother has just taken it out of the oven."

It made me quietly steam, the way Ma knocked herself out with that bread. And expected me to act like getting it delivered was a sacred trust. Brother! Nobody was a tin god to me just because they were summer people. All it takes to own a Cadillac is a few thousand dollars.

Actually, they must have had their stupid side. The way they used to let their help get away with robbery. We ate the Ogdens' sugar and lard and stuff all winter in the g.o.d.'s. And one year when Dad chauffeured for them, we rode on their tires. Our car took the same size.

But try to argue with my mother. They were summer people, so they were a breed apart, even if they didn't furnish free rides anymore.

Dad was almost as bad, in a different sort of way. Naturally, knowing Pappy, his way would have to be a little bit different to make it worthwhile. I wouldn't want to say Dad was exactly lazy, but he didn't especially enjoy working. All those summers when he was gardener around the Ogdens just got him in the habit of never doing anything in an hour that he could drag out to half a day. Actually he made a lot more money after he started lobster fishing, but it wasn't as much fun. There wasn't anybody to fool but himself.

That was all there was to that, so I headed Francis down toward the Lighthouse. Susan was always taking walks by herself, and she had a favorite place down on the rocks. Sometimes she would sit down there and write a poem in the back of her English Lit notebook. About the water or the rocks or the Lighthouse or something. I was the only one she read them to.

The longest was one she wrote about her aunt and visiting day at school. She hadn't told her aunt about visiting day when all the parents were supposed to come, because she knew she would wear this black taffeta dress that Mrs. Ogden had given her, and black silk stockings with it, and she would look old and sort of shrunken beside most of the kids' parents, even if she knew more than any of them. Susan didn't read that one to me. I saw it by accident one day when her notebook was lying open.

It was all about how much she loved Mrs. Becker even if she couldn't ever say so and was ashamed of being ashamed of her and couldn't ever forget how she had hurt her even if Mrs. Becker didn't know it, just by feeling that way. It was pretty good because it made me feel bad too. I respected Mrs. Becker even if she didn't like me much. She was really a worthwhile person, one of the few I ever met.

But what I mean, that was Susan for you. Instead of putting a thing like that down to profit and loss, she would keep it mulling away inside her for a year or two.

I left Francis by the boathouse and took the path through the woods across the point. It was quiet in there, and damp, with big orange mushrooms growing. Poisonous ones. Then under the quiet I began to hear the ocean, not any special sound, just a swallowed roar.

In a minute I caught a glimpse of Susan's head in the sunshine just beyond the end of the bushes. Then, believe me, I nearly fainted, because there was a fellow sitting out there on the rocks with her. And practically a stranger at that.

His name was Hine Hanscomb and all I knew about him was some story that he had left his wife—they lived in Providence or Pawtucket or someplace—so he was here visiting a cousin. He was about my height, shorter than Susan, and his body was real slight, like a boy's. But when you saw his face, it was old as the hills.

He looked like somebody you might see in the movies. His eyes were big and dark with lovely long lashes and his face was long and thin with sort of an anguished expression, but wide at the top with nice wavy dark hair. Someone said his wife got tired of supporting him. It seems he was a real smart boy in the upper story and he was going to start magazines and write books and reorganize the advertising business, amongst other things.

But all his big schemes piddled down to having a story published in some magazine no one ever heard of. That was what I heard anyhow, and it was supposed to come from his cousin.

And there he sat with Susan just as though they were old pals. Unless you knew Susan you wouldn't realize how sensational that was. It took her years to get friendly with anyone, usually. Which led me to the thought of how I'd love to be a little bird listening to that conversation. It was bound to be educational.

The next best thing seemed to be to get up close and linger in the bushes. As luck would have it there was just a little speck of breeze coming my way.

He was doing the talking naturally, giving her those big brown eyes as though she was Marilyn Monroe. His picking out Susan of all people to throw a line at was so ludicrous I almost collapsed.

"I could tell you things about yourself right now, Susan, you don't even know. When somebody interests me I can read them the way other people read a book. It's my business. If you're going to write about the world and the people in it, you've got to know what makes them tick...."

Well! I eased down on a little hillock of grass and got comfortable and lighted a cigarette. This was certainly nothing I wanted to miss. It was going to enlarge my fountain of knowledge, by leaps and bounds.

She was laughing in a sort of flustered way, but she was interested. I guess he didn't realize what a miracle he was performing.

Her hair was just glistening in the sun. She had jet-black curly hair I would have given my eyeteeth for, but she didn't do anything but have it whacked off straight across in bangs, and short just below her ears. She was so funny and shy about how she looked that you might think she was homely but she wasn't.

At school in the john when she started combing her hair in front of the mirror and anyone came in, she left right off no matter how it looked and went out. It's as though she got self-conscious to see herself fixing herself as someone else saw her. She wouldn't even look in the mirror unless she was alone; then she could spend plenty of time at it.

Even with me she was like that. If I said, "You want my lipstick, Sue?" she'd pretend she didn't hear, and walk off so I couldn't ask her again.

The kid was so shy some ways like that she didn't seem hardly human. It was all mixed up with her feeling she wasn't like the others at school—which she wasn't, God knows—fooling around and petting and thinking anyone must be sick to sit at home for an evening reading a book. She didn't play basketball either. Mrs. Becker didn't think she was strong enough, so she missed a lot, going out of town to games and the high old time afterward in some joint. Charlie and I were both on the varsity teams so we had ourselves a real ball.

Of course the Ogdens being so fond of Mrs. Becker and eating there all summer, they used to have Susan over to their house, and that's where she picked up some of her peculiar ideas. She played cribbage with Reverend Ogden to relax his mental state after writing a sermon, and Odessa was always giving her books to look at and stuff, and talking about brainy subjects.

Hine was really wound up sitting out on those rocks. I guess he wasn't used to so much air and sunshine, because he kept sniffing around with a sort of suspicious look. Probably expected the woods to be full of bears and panthers. But it didn't slow up his tongue.

"You need the city, Susan, I could see that the minute I spotted you—at that stupid dance or hop or whatever it was. My God, I never saw such a bunch of cattle in my life, all dressed up and fattened like beef for the market. Horsing around under those crepe-paper streamers. My God. You want to know something? You looked out of place! You know why? You've got something different, in your face, in the way you move, even in that dress you had on. Where'd you get that? Not around here."

"Someone sent it to me."

She *had* looked nice in that dress, though it was pretty simple beside most of the others. White with blue polka dots. Old lady Ogden sent it from Boston.

At that point I got so unnerved at his picking Susan out of all the kids in town that I dropped my cigarette stub and almost started a forest fire. Trying to stamp it out without a racket, I almost choked from having to laugh so hard.

Naturally he was getting around to making a pass, but she was such a damn innocent it would probably come as a complete surprise. That began to worry me on top of everything else.

"You know what New York would do for you?" He never stopped talking a minute, but I can't go into all of it. Anyhow, in New York, she would be able to breathe and stretch and take great bites of life or something, gulp it in until she wanted to burst, and what she needed was a cold-water flat with cockroaches running over the floor and vitality oozing out of her pores and his pores and everyone's they came in contact with, who would all be painters and writers and general queers, all poor but happy with their art, no, not happy, God no, he caught that back right away, not happy, but feeling the shape of reality and the true urgency of love and physical need—I knew he would get there sooner or later—and taking their punishment for being the only ones who really knew what life was all about, and lived it and talked it and dissected it. On and on and on.

I smoked about half the cigarettes and my head was aching, but I was sort of hypnotized.

She needed to look at pictures, among other things, and he was going to take her around places where their feet would clank on the marble floors and he would get a great bang out of watching her face when she looked at something or other and this and that, I couldn't say what, and then afterward to rest their feet they would sit in some little cafe and eat Hungarian hominy or Armenian oysters or Irish jelly beans, they were never going to have anything like a hot dog and a Coca-Cola, believe me, and then back in the Village—this was in the city but it turns out to be a Village, small world!—they would have lively long evenings with a lot of other offbeat characters talking themselves hoarse proclaiming the laws of the universe, and what ailed them, and having big fights about who was saner, Van Go or several other excitable types who had dandy times slicing off their ears or their cuticles or something and mailing them about the country.

That nearly finished me. I began to laugh and hiccough with my head rolled up in Charlie's jacket, thrashing around in my little nest like a madwoman. Susan would probably be wondering if cuticles was a naughty word.

He had a gift all right. I never heard so many words roll out of one human being in my life. And our Susie was lapping it up. For another thing, of course, he was the only guy who had ever paid her strict attention like that, analyzing her inner workings and so on.

She was really beginning to relax. First thing I knew she was letting him read a poem she had just written. Naturally he gave it a big deal, hitching up close to point out a line or a word or something with his arm against her shoulder.

I decided for her sake things had gone far enough, and anyhow my legs were broken and my neck was stiff. So I crawled out of my den and crippled back up the path a little way to make a formal announcement that I was coming.

Hine looked about as welcoming as a thunderstorm, but Susan was tickled to death. It must have been sort of a strain on her, not being used to it.

"What d'ya know! Hope I didn't interrupt anything."

I gave him just a bare flicker to see if he was still alive after the oration. But he wasn't in the mood and said he had to tear along, giving Susan a long intense look as though they were old chums and I was some one-legged jail bird.

"Well!" I said after he'd gone, "what's this, a new romance? Didn't I ever tell you what the city slicker did to the farmer's daughter?"

As a matter of fact I felt very grandmotherly, as though I ought to tell her the facts of life, and on the other hand, not many guys turn me down so cold. In favor of Susan. What an odd crimp he must be.

"No, and don't." She was really on her high horse.

"Wait till Edgar hears!"

At school it had to be someone, like Charlie and Evelyn, so it was Susan and Edgar. Edgar was all right, he was just someone you never noticed, and I think the only reason Susan went around with him was because he never bothered her, beyond holding hands and kissing her good-night on the doorstep with his mouth shut. I mean she was fond of him, he was a good kid, one of the good ones who never swear or steal pencils at Tucker's or play with naughty little girls when they start getting interested in their anatomy. His mother had him where it hurt, so he took Susan to the dances and walked her home after basketball games.

It was anguishing to see them dancing. She was a good dancer, very graceful, and he was awful. He joggled up and down and hunched his shoulders. Plenty of times I've watched her across the floor when they were jiggling along like tiddlywinks to the music, and it was no picnic. She was just lasting it out, wondering what all the fun was about, where all the excitement was, and the big kick other kids got.

If you want to get mucky it was pretty sad, but she was so darned touchy you couldn't help. Except that it always helped a little if I was there, though God knows how I guessed that, it was never from anything she said.

"Hears what?" She was practically pleased with herself, she was so charged up. "You want me to read you what I wrote this morning?"

"Suit yourself." Two could play at this game, but it was no fun because right away all the wind went out of her sails. "Naturally as the first and fondest admirer of your poetic genius I expect to hear," I said crossly.

She perked up and this was the poem, don't ask me why.

Gulls on the flats
That the seas rolled back
Crying their baby's rasp
Retreating, renewing
Webbed feet in the mud
White sides in the sun
Heavily rising

Miriam Colwell

And rapidly swooping
Gliding and dipping
Shrieking and swooping
Blown on the air's ebb
Settling with wings upspread
Feet in the muck
Of the outgoing tide.

"Swell," I said. "That's really good, Sue."

All of a sudden I felt very restless. The morning had worn me down.

"Let's go up to town and see a movie, Sue," I said. "Lord, I'm tired and sick of this dump."

It all closed in on me, how really sick and tired of it I was, the orders and the same old faces, the same old wisecracks, and the whole stretch of empty road staring me in the face now school was over. I was the candidate for a change, a real sea-going, rip-roaring change of scenery, but there was the blasted forty-two bucks I owed Ma, and where was I going to head for anyhow?

"Come on! If I sit here another minute I'm going to curl up and die."

"I haven't got a cent," she said very seriously.

She was always serious about money, as though you either had some or you didn't, which was a very negative attitude. But she would go, because she thought the sun rose and set at my suggestion.

"Come on," I said. "Love will find a way."

Francis was waiting and away we started. Neither of us was exactly dressed for town. I had on my old white sneakers and striped light and dark gray pedal-pushers which were pretty dirty, plus Charlie's jacket, bright green with orange trim and gold letters. Susan was wearing a tweed skirt she'd had forever and before that was Odessa Ogden's, and a white sweater that had shrunk so she had to push up the sleeves and keep hauling it down at the waist.

We should have found a busy street and begun a singing act, the Starving Orphans' Duet, with a tambourine for people to throw money in. But I didn't think of it then.

What I did think of was a bottle of apricot nectar that Charlie had hidden last night on our way home. It was about five miles up on the turnpike, in a clump of alders near a dead birch without any limbs. We had marked the birch with a secret mark. I had marked it standing on Charlie's shoulders so it would be high up, and as he stood six feet three, it was.

I spotted the tree. You couldn't miss with that big red chalk swastika, and after a half-hour's tramping around, Susan stumbled over the bottle.

By that time we were sorely in need of nourishment, so we sat there taking turns, with the cars going by, whoosh, whoosh, and Francis shaking in his shoes. It was quite hot just sitting, but the pine trees smelled wonderful in the sun, and we counted to see who could get the most out-of-state license numbers.

When the last drop had dribbled down our throats we felt quite revived.

I said, "Come on, Susie, let's retire into the bushes before we move on."

I only said this to see how horrified she could look. One of the dear girl's real panics was to have anyone suspect her of owning kidneys. At school the johns had just partial doors, from the knee to the neck, depending on how tall you were; and as Susan was taller than me and could pretty well see out over the darned things, she seemed to think everyone could see in just as well.

It's a wonder that girl hadn't burst. One fall a whole bunch of us went to the County Fair, and naturally the time came when we went to find the little-girls' room. Susan and I walked in together.

It was one big room with a row of open-holers all around the walls, and about a dozen women were present. They all looked up when we came in, and one old lady grinned and said, "Here's a couple of vacancies, girls!"

I thought Susan would die right there. She made a funny gurgling noise and would have rushed right out except that more customers were crowding in, clogging the door, so she stood there trying to hide behind me and not look at anyone.

She managed to get out, though, in a minute or two, and I guess she tramped ten miles trying to find a spot of cover.

She never knew what she missed. It was a real educational experience. I couldn't tear myself away. There wasn't anything on the Midway half as interesting. The knotholes some of those characters must have crawled out of, and the language they used, you wouldn't believe. For odd types, Hollywood could have cast their pictures for the next twenty years. You had a psychological study any way you looked.

The old lady and I had quite a conversation. She told all about her son who was in jail and how hard it was on his family of about ten kids all under five years of age and what a good boy he was, only never quite right in the head. I told her my father was serving a fifty-year sentence for raping a movie star when he worked in Hollywood as a scene painter, and how Ma went to her and begged for the sake of me and my brothers to forgive him, and how they both broke down and cried on each other's shoulders and agreed boys would be boys, so we expected Pa home any day now, for good behavior.

We were old buddies by the time I left. She outstayed me. I guess her feet were tired.

So I left Susan in the car delicately averting her head. It's funny the way things come to you sometimes, but while we were sitting there it came to me that Charlie and I were through. It was the way some mornings you get up feeling lousy, only without anything really being the matter, then sooner or later you begin to sneeze or get a terrific backache and that was the trouble.

Probably I woke up knowing we were washed up, and that was one reason my nerves were so frayed, but I didn't know I knew it until we were drinking his nasty old apricot nectar. Oh, there wouldn't be any shattering scene. He would be around every week or so when he could get off, and maybe once in a while he would convince me that the old black magic had us in its spell again, but the sad fact was, Evelyn and Charlie had graduated. It was in the cards. Life was going to be different from now on.

His mother never liked me anyhow. She was about as heart-warming as the girl on the Old Dutch Cleanser can. The kind that thinks it's terribly stimulating to have someone read a book review at the Woman's Club, preferably herself.

If she knew Charlie like I knew Charlie, the old girl would have turned up her toes. We both had a big hand in his education. She taught him to shake hands and open doors and get up when ladies entered and pass around cups at her tea parties so that all the guests said, "Isn't Charles a dear charming boy! Such lovely manners."

I taught him plenty of other things, which I'll bet he won't forget either. But anyhow, this was my fare-thee-well to Tomcat, whether he ever knew it or not. And old Heartburn, his mother, could be terribly, terribly relieved that little Evelyn had no intention of waiting around with her fingers crossed in the hope of marrying her precious son.

When we bowled on, like a man with one leg shorter than the other, one wheel over on the shoulder and one down on the pavement—Francis insisted on going that way because all the fast drivers made him nervous—and the apricot nectar making a lovely little warm spot in my tummy, I felt ready to cope with the big problem of money.

There was a slight possibility roaming around in the back of my head. It was something Charlie and I had stumbled on when we were out selling ads for our school paper. We got very hungry one day, and right out of the blue it occurred to me how easy it would be just to sell a few extra ads.

Naturally you couldn't do this too close to home, but if you were far enough away they never saw the paper anyhow. The storekeepers just took ads to help out school kids, not because they ever thought it would improve business. Most of them had never heard of the *Sentinel*. They were just too good-natured to say no.

It worked like a charm, and Charlie and I went to the Hotel Ambershire and had roast duckling, with cold soup to start and peaches on sort of cookies for dessert. Three bucks apiece. If you don't make the most of human nature, somebody else will.

Just outside of town a few miles, there were a lot of stores stringing along, big furniture places, and hand-sewn-moccasin shops, and some junky restaurants, plus a big hardware store which I had marked as a good prospect.

When we got there I reined Francis in and we rolled slowly to rest in front of this big plate-glass window full of lawn mowers and garden hose and wheelbarrows, with Francis's reflection like a scared little jackrabbit right in the middle.

"What you say we go in here, Susie, and sell them an ad in the *Sentinel*?"

"But it was published a month ago," she said, as though I hadn't heard. After all, I was the assistant editor-in-chief.

"*I* know it, stupid. But they don't."

"Oh Evelyn, I don't think we ought to."

"Okay. Stay out here then. I'm going to."

She tagged along. She hated to miss anything, though sometimes you wouldn't have believed it.

The store was roughly the size of a basketball court inside, but the minute I spotted an old guy patting lily bulbs in a wicker basket, I knew we were on the right trail. He was the owner, but his nephew in the back ran the place, as he himself was addled most of the time from drinking gin. From eight o'clock in the morning on. Charles's father was a fifth cousin or something, but he didn't like them because they never gave him any discount.

I switched on a big smile for the old geezer, giving him plenty of hip action as we walked the half-acre or so of store to where he was.

"Mr. Swazy?"

"Yes. Yes, indeed, young lady." His little bloodshot eyes gave me an inventory that didn't miss a thing.

"We're selling space in our school paper, the *Sentinel* from Rutabagus High." I made up the Rutabagus on the spur of the moment, thinking it was just as well not to be too definite. "And we just need one more ad to fill it, Mr. Swazy. It's three dollars for the space, really a wonderful buy considering all the people who see it. You can say anything you want or just print your name."

"What's the matter you're so late getting around, young lady? Why, you're a couple weeks behind the times."

The old fox was pretty keen this morning. Susan didn't bat an eye. She was very trustworthy that way, and put on a look of great respectability and began to pat a cat that came up. She was crazy about cats anyway, and puppies. Big dogs scared her to death.

"Yes, we are late, Mr. Swazy," I said, letting my voice tremble and giving him a high-voltage charge through my lashes. "You see, our principal got polio and had to be put in an oxygen tent and the whole school was closed down for a month. We were all crazy about Mr. Shaw and nobody would go back until we knew he was going to live. We went on sort of a sit-down strike and the School Committee couldn't do a thing. We forfeited our basketball games and everything. It was pretty grim. That's why we're so late graduating and getting out our paper. I realize we're way behind everyone else. Well, I don't want to take your time, Mr. Swazy . . ."

I pretended my feelings were hurt and I was going to walk right out of there, and he got so excited he grabbed my arm.

"Wait! Wait a minute, young lady. I didn't say I wasn't willing to help out. I'm always willing to help out a pretty girl."

That was no news to me. Most men were.

"What school did you say this was?"

"It's just a small high, Mr. Swazy. You know where Cottonwood Corner is, don't you? It's down near there. On the other side of Cape Porpoise."

If he did know he was the only person living as far as I knew, but it's all in your point of view. Maybe he did.

"Why, yes, yes, in a general way." He was warming up fast where my arm was concerned. "Look here, girlie, how's for a bargain? You come on in my office and keep me company while I take my medicine—got a bad ticker, see, got to tend to it every hour on the dot—and we can tend to the details in there. Tell your friend she can wait right here and play with kitty cat."

What an old mealymouth he was. He had some details in mind too. I let him drag me a few feet just to whet his appetite.

His nephew had his eye on us across the pasture and I figured he wouldn't let it go too far. He didn't.

"What's the matter, Uncle Raymond?" he bellowed. "Anything I can do?" And over he came at a fast trot.

Uncle Raymond was doing all right. His pasty old face got red as a beet. "No need to bother. No need to bother you, Bill. This young lady and I are transacting a little business, that's all. I can tend to it. We'll just step into the office for a minute . . ."

But Bill was right in the way, bless his name, and stood there. He was fat in the rear and nearsighted, but he knew the score. "No need to trouble, Uncle Raymond," just as though he wasn't gritting his teeth. "Let me take care of it for you. How much, young lady?"

"It's only three dollars. How do you want it to read?"

He gave me a look that said, Don't think I'm that stupid, and grunted, "Swazy and Swazy, Hardware," handing me three lovely new bills as though they burned his fingers.

"Thanks a million, Uncle Raymond," I said, giving the poor old disappointed duck my best girlish grateful smile, and wasted no time departing, practically having to drag Susan who kept whispering about the damned cat being thin and pregnant.

"Call the Society for Unwed Mothers," I said, "we've got plenty of money." Not that I didn't sympathize, I'm very fond of animals, but it was no place to linger longer.

We decided on the Strand Theatre because the seats are more comfortable than at the Royal, and the Orpheum where they have double features always smells like dirty feet. The Strand popcorn is better too.

Before we got there, though, Francis began to cough and shudder so we turned right in to a Flying Red Horse. It's very convenient to have money. Many's the night we limped home from town by stopping at every gas station, after closing time, and emptying the hoses. Gas attendants are very wasteful about draining their gas hoses.

"Big day for Francis!" Susan said. "Five whole gallons."

We each got a Coca-Cola out of the machine to soothe our nerves. The boy who put in the gas was cute, dark blond hair that stood up in a peak and greenish eyes.

He cleaned and cleaned at the windshield trying to hear what we were arguing about, which was the color of his eyes, until Susan got nervous for fear I'd decide to make a date with him and leave her wandering around alone, which naturally hadn't entered my head. Or what she was more afraid of was that he'd have a friend and she would have to sink or swim with him in the backseat. Her big trouble was lack of confidence.

To ease her mind I handed him the money like Mrs. Astor tipping her lackey, and said, "Compliments of Crazy Swazy, Lunatics and Lardware," which made her start giggling.

Susan had a very infectious giggle; it started at the bottom and ran up the scale, and in a minute our eyes were streaming. Cutie Pie just stood there looking forlorn—he had wonderful hips—until a grimy character covered with grease spots appeared from inside and said, "You're stopping up the pump, girls. If you want to throw fits, go up the road to the Gulf Station."

"Oh, lay an egg, and see if you can't cackle," I said to him, and Francis went roaring out of there leaving a nice cloud of his exhaust. People who try to be fresh get my goat.

In the lobby we bought popcorn and salted peanuts and two Mounds apiece, and I must say we were a pretty comical pair in the big mirror that lines one wall. I hitched up my pedal-pushers and stuck my tail out and my tummy in, ignoring the usher who was giving us his attention. Crummy uniforms never impressed me. Susan just shuddered when she caught sight of us and slunk along behind me, pretending she wasn't there.

Once inside where it was dim we felt better, and sailed down the aisle all ready to enjoy ourselves. We tried out four locations before we found the perfect one, it was only the Eyes and Ears of the World anyhow, and at least six weeks old, but one or two soreheads in the back began to growl, "Sit down," "Make up your mind," and so on. Isn't it a fact this world is full of soreheads. Probably turned their mother's milk to vinegar.

The movie was about the circus, God help us. Big deal. The only one bearable was Cornel Wilde, and he was but dreamy when he drove up in a little foreign convertible and got out in his tights. What a build on that boy! But he got hurt and reduced to a peanut vendor.

It went on and on and on like that until I thought death and taxes were going to have to move over and make room for one more. If you want to look at animals go to a zoo is my advice. Even Cornel got disgusted. My can was aching before it was a quarter through. Susan went to sleep. Anyhow, when it finally ended for lack of absolutely nothing else they could think of, we were so stiff we had to help each other up the aisle and to the Ladies like a pair of cripples.

We were certainly a pair. Susan looked as though she hadn't been in bed all night, and I looked as though I might have been all day. Both of us as pale as washed-out oysters.

"They must of run out of film in Hollywood," I said, "otherwise, why stop?"

"I'm hungry," Susan said, and she was so worn down she started combing her hair just as if I wasn't there.

"Hungry? I'm *starving!*" Now that she mentioned it I had never been so hungry in my entire life. Fifteen cents.

"We could get a hamburger and divide it," she said with a sort of hollow laugh.

"Oh my God, Sue, a hamburger. I could eat five."

Nothing makes me as hungry as eating popcorn. I should have known better. She looked so woebegone I had to pep up and pretend to have plans.

"Look, we can't go all the way home as hungry as we are."

"What can we *do?*"

"Well, *think*," I said. "You're supposed to be the big brain around here. Exercise it, for heaven's sake."

"How much for a package of doughnuts at the A & P? There's twelve in a package, and they might be giving away samples of something."

"I couldn't care less," I said in disgust. "We need a *meal.* It must be three o'clock. My God, I haven't eaten all day, not even breakfast."

Outside it was bright and sunny, which made matters worse. Who wants to give up the battle and go home at that hour of the day? *Anything* can happen and frequently does. In fact, my motto was: meet happenchance halfway. Home may be where the heart is, but it's also where to go when you can't go somewhere else.

There sat Francis as smug as a Cadillac with five gallons of gas sloshing around inside him and here we were, weak from hunger. The street was full of traffic and shoppers, and everyone had a real cheerful expression as though they had just gotten up from fried oysters or hot roast pork with gravy, or even a club sandwich. It was enough to try the patience of a saint.

Susan got in her side and slouched down without a word. When I was aggravated she always got very depressed. The Kools were still in my pocket so I tossed them in her lap. "Got them for you this morning on the way over."

"You *did!*" She was so overcome at my thoughtfulness that she almost forgot our big dilemma. "Golly, thanks; you have one too."

A Kool on an empty stomach was not my idea of solid comfort, but not to hurt her feelings I took one. Then I thought if we talked about something an idea might come to me quicker.

"Sue," I said, to my complete surprise, "do you like Hine Hanscomb?"

She sat up as though I had pinched her, and looked out the window. "Don't be silly. Look at the jet up there, can you see it? Up over the water tower. They make me nervous roaring around so close. Do they make you nervous, Ev?"

"That guy Hine makes me nervous," I said. "You listen to your old Aunt Evelyn and have very little to do with that character."

"You don't like him because he hasn't made a pass at you."

That nearly knocked me. "Oh baby doll! *That* jerk?"

She couldn't look at me after that crack, just kept staring at the people going by. What odd notions she could cook up in that black head of hers! I started to say a number of things but it didn't seem worth it. Anyone else I would have laid out in lavender, believe me.

"It's none of my business," I said in a very cool tone, "just I had thought we were close friends, going through school together and all that. Heavens, the last thing I want to do, Susan, is push my nose in your business. Ex*cuse* me."

That brought her around in jig time. Her eyes are brown, sometimes black, and they got all misty, and her face, which is sort of thin with a nice mouth, turned real white.

"Oh Evelyn, you know I . . . you know you . . . we *are* . . . please don't be cross . . . you know I . . ."

Translated, this meant, we *were* best friends, she felt closer to me than anyone, she told me things and showed me her poems and stuff that she didn't anyone else. But, believe me, her saying that really got a rise. I didn't know she had so much varnish.

"I've got nothing against him, Sue," I said. "Honest. Except he's pretty old, and, I don't know, it's just a feeling . . ."

"But you're always after me to go out with someone—Joe, or that trumpet player, or someone." She sounded sad, and a little mad at the same time.

"Oh forget it. Forget I ever said a word. Look, it's just a feeling I got I can't explain. Only take it easy, kid. And listen, anyhow, he's a married man."

She began to laugh. There was nothing wrong with Susan's sense of humor. "You're a fine one to sound so moral. Okay. I won't make a move without consulting you, Mrs. Anthony. Golly, I'm so *hungry.*"

If my nervous system hadn't been so jangled with all that crawling around in the bushes, and arguing with Sue, and the movie, I would never have gone to the Blue Bottle. But in my state of mind, there was no room for half measures.

"I know where I can get some money," I said, giving Francis due warning that we were about to amble on. He always had to have a few minutes to accustom his old bones to the thought that the day was not yet done.

Susan looked puzzled and lighted us another Kool.

"I've got a friend across town," I said. "He owns the Blue Bottle bar and he'll let me have some money."

"He will?" she said, as happy as a clam again. "And we can pay him back next time we come up."

That made me hoot. Sometimes she could think up the weirdest things. "This guy don't play that way, honey lamb," I said, and let her ponder that in her pure little brain.

The Blue Bottle was down by the river, across from the railroad station, and it had an old oak stand-up bar with a footrail and sawdust on the floor. So many tourists kept sending their friends there for the atmosphere that most of the atmosphere moved down the street to the joint under the barbershop. Mac had blue lights above the booths, and a couple of Negro boys to serve drinks and fill the popcorn bowls.

He was loaded with money, more money than brains. I was there the first time when Mr. Booth, our basketball coach, and his wife took Charlie and me to a college basketball game at the University. They stopped in there for a nightcap on the way home. Charlie and I had Cokes, being innocent youth, and athletes in the bargain.

In Science class the next morning, Mr. Booth came over to my desk and whispered, Did I have a hangover? with a big grin. I whispered back, No, just constipation, which fixed him.

Mac came over to our table that night. He and Mrs. Booth once went to Sunday School together or something. He wore a nifty pinstripe dark blue suit, and a big gold band on his left hand; and he told all about his wife, and working in his garden, big family-type, but brother, he gave me the eye a couple of times, and I said to myself, Dearie, this is no gentleman to be backed into a corner by. I mean, you can tell.

After that, whenever I saw him around, he made a big hello and joked about being sure to drop in whenever we were selling tickets or magazine subscriptions or anything.

"Give an old man a break," he always said, with a toothy smile.

When he opened his mouth wide enough you could see a diamond set in gold in the front of one of his upper teeth. Anyone who can stand that much punishment had my admiration. I die every time I even think of going to the dentist.

Naturally as long as he wanted to be a sucker we gave him plenty of opportunity. Charlie tagged along with me, though. He bought ten tickets to the Senior play and then told us to give them to our relatives, and he gave twenty-five dollars to our scholarship fund. But he always managed to let me know it would have been lots more fun if I'd come alone. Lots more exercise too.

Sooner or later, though, I knew I had to see who was smarter, him or me, and right then seemed the time. We were going to perish of starvation anyhow, if something wasn't done.

"You stay here with Francis," I said to Susan. "I won't be any longer than I can help."

She never minded waiting like that. You know why? She liked to watch the people go by. It was a shame to waste money on a movie ticket for that girl; she had more fun slouched down in Francis, just watching people walk up and down the street. Some fun. It takes very little to entertain some people.

So I brushed my hair up and put on more lipstick and went toddling into the Blue Bottle, as big as life and twice as natural.

One of the boys was behind the bar and he gave me a very strange look.

As a matter of fact he was a pretty cool kid, but I had other fish to fry, so I just asked for Mac. It wasn't a drinking time of day, thank goodness, and there was just one old wreck down at the far end glowering into his beer. Maybe he thought I came from Alcoholics Anonymous or something to lure him out of there.

He couldn't have been more wrong. I wouldn't have lured a hair off his head, even for his widowed mother.

"Well, hello!" Mac said. "This *is* a surprise. Come over and sit down where it's quiet. What'll you have to cool your thirst?"

"A beer would taste awfully good," I said, and steered him toward a booth with a big bowl of potato chips.

"Well, how's your life, Evelyn?" he waved an arm at the bar boy as though I was a movie queen instead of in my crummy pedal-pushers. "All through school, huh? Well, you'll always have those years to look back on. Nothing like them."

He wore a blue tie to match his eyes, and a blue and white striped shirt, and a gray flannel suit. Very sharp. It's too bad he was so old and lecherous. Otherwise he wasn't bad.

The boy brought two big beers, all beaded with cold and with just enough head. They were strictly luscious-looking, and to keep from diving in too fast I took a big handful of potato chips.

"Look, Mr. MacCaster, I don't want to take up your time if you're busy."

"You don't?" he said. "I was hoping you did, Evelyn. I was hoping we were going to sit here and have a nice friendly visit and get a little bit acquainted. I've been interested in you for a long time, you know that?"

There was no sense evading the issue, so I looked him straight in his blue eyes with both barrels. It's so easy to get a man excited, like sticking pins in a baby.

"You *have* been, Mr. MacCaster?"

"How about calling me Mac, Evelyn? Don't we know each other well enough for that? After all I'm old enough to be your father, dear."

He said it, I didn't.

"Oh Mr. MacCaster, I mean, Mac, don't say a thing like that."

We had another heart-to-heart look and his hand was trembling so he could hardly lift his beer.

"My God, Evelyn. Dear. Listen, it's stuffy in here, dear. God! How about just a little ride to cool us off? My car's right out the back."

His knees were beginning to play tag, but I've played that before.

"Oh Mac, I couldn't, honestly, I'd like to, but I've got a girlfriend waiting outside. I just wanted to stop in to say hello. I don't know why. I guess I shouldn't have. She's starving, too . . . I really can't stay but a shake."

"A girlfriend?" His mouth closed up as though he had bit on a sour pickle. His lips were quite thin and his skin over his cheekbones was drawn real tight. Then his temples were hollowed out with blue veins. His face really fascinated me.

"Look Evelyn, I thought we were going to have a nice get-together, dear. Want another beer? Hey, Bradley! Don't make yourself sick on those damned potato chips."

It was mean to leave poor old Susan out there, but what could I do? She would sure have spoiled the party. I didn't know yet how I was going to work this out, but while I was debating, those potato chips saved the day. That was a big item right there in his favor. They were elegant potato chips, and believe me, I've been served some rancid stale old potato chips.

I decided the time had come to lay my cards on the table. "My girlfriend and I went to the movies, Mac," I said, as though he was the last friend I hoped to see in this life, "and when we came out, we were so hungry. Honest, doesn't it make you ravenous to go to the movies? And we couldn't decide what to do, buy a hamburger and split it between us or what, and just then we were going past here, and I said, I'm going in to say hello to Mr. MacCaster, no matter what—"

"For Christ's sake, honey," he said, "what do you mean, you got no money between you? Why didn't you say so? I thought we were old friends, dear."

He deserved another warming-up for that, so we just sat and looked at each other for about five minutes and I let him hug one ankle with his foot. I was getting into the spirit of things.

"I think I'd like that," I said very throatily, as though I just couldn't help myself. Being old friends.

"God damn it. God damn it." He was so fidgety now I was afraid he would spill his beer all over that beautiful gray flannel jacket, so I moved it away. He caught my hand as though it was a lovely womanly gesture.

"Come for a ride, Evelyn, just a little ride. God, dear, you want to be good to an old man, don't you? You know how much it would please me, don't you, Evelyn? Look, we'll only be gone fifteen minutes, I swear it to God. Just so we get a breath of air together. Jesus, Evelyn, you don't need to be afraid of going with *me, you* know that. *Don't* you, dear? You know I wouldn't harm a hair of your head." He began to groan very softly, as though I was pinching his vitals. It was a pretty good stunt, considering. He was no slouch in the excite department.

"I want you to drive my Caddy," he muttered. We were very nose to nose by this time as though the joint was full of people trying to overhear us. "See how you like it. Maybe you'll want to borrow it sometimes when you're around town, if you like the way she drives."

What a smart cookie he was. All of a sudden he pretended to cool off, stopped rubbing my ankle, and straightened his jacket as though he was talking to a parent-teachers' meeting.

He dragged a thin alligator billfold out of his pocket and eased out a ten-dollar bill where I could see it.

"Could you and your friend get a good meal downtown on that, dear? Look, I want you to come to old Mac when you're in a spot like this, let him feel he's a friend of yours. You know what, dear, after you and me take a breath of air to see how you like the new Caddy, I'm just going to slip this right into the pocket of your, er . . . blazer there, and no questions asked. No strings. Just a token from an old guy that thinks you're all right, thinks you're pretty special, wants you to be happy. What do you say, dear? My God, how your eyes shine. What I'd give to be your age again—just for a night, Evelyn! How about it, would we make a night of it, two old pals together? God, the fun we could have. Well, dear, I'm not going to urge you to humor an old duffer. We've been right out in the open with each other. If you don't want to go, okay. You walk right out that front door, dear, and we'll let bygones be bygones."

He leaned back, fastening his jacket, with that blue hand-painted tie sparking up his eyes, and a real cold grin on his lips. Right then I could have reached across the table and choked him with my bare hands, because so far the score was on his side, and little Evelyn was not one to lose without a fight.

I had to go another quarter and tie things up. Who was smarter, him or me? Well, come on, brother, we were wasting time.

"I've always wanted to drive a Cadillac," I said, and I got up and walked across that damned empty sawdusted dismal blue room to the back, just as though I didn't know Bradley and that dummy rummy weren't turned around watching, sniggering in their whiskers and making bets on how long it would take, and admiring the smart outfit I was wearing, sneakers and all.

God, sometimes I hate women just a little more than I hate men.

The car was a convertible, light gray with a navy top, about thirty feet long. When he held the door for me to slide in under the wheel, a small doubt lodged in my windpipe and stayed there. That seat was big enough to bed down a couple of giants like the Ogdens. Maybe I wasn't such a smart cookie, after all.

Just then Bradley poked his head out and said, "The Schenley salesman's here to see you, Mister Mac."

Mac was just getting in. He turned around and believe me, he looked murderous, spiffy tie and all.

"Tell him to wait," he growled. "Give him some of that brandy under the counter. I'll be right back."

Just the same, I felt better. He couldn't fool around forever with someone waiting for him, and after all, I was driving. That was the first point on my side. The second one was after I had started the motor and poked at a button to see what it was, lights or ham and eggs or plumbing or what.

That nice navy top just rose right up off our heads and settled back like a bird into its nest.

"Oh!" I said. "Isn't that *won*derful, Mac!" He looked a lot less than ecstatic, but what could he say? It was a warm summer day, any cluck would want the top down on a convertible, and there we were right smack out in the open.

I felt better and better. The car was a dream to handle, not that I'd ever say so before Francis. It was pretty stimulating, purring off down the street like Doris Duke and all her millions.

Mac sat there looking glum. I guess he didn't like all that sun on his head. His hair was getting thin on the top. Maybe he was thinking about the salesman and hoping Schenley wouldn't be jumping the price the longer he waited in that gloomy old cave, while the boss was off tomcatting.

"Turn left here, *here*, dear!" he shouted all of a sudden. I guess he had expected the Caddy would turn there all by herself, or else he really thought I was ripe for a tête-à-tête.

This town was no big mystery to me; I knew the way out to River Park as well as he did. So I turned right, smack into the one-way traffic pouring down Market Street.

When I saw his face, I wailed, "Oh, wasn't that the way you meant, Mac? I never can remember left from right."

He put his left hand on my knee and began to check whether all the bones were there or not. "Dear, you turned *right*."

"Oh Mac, I'm sorry."

The same way I was sorry to have to stop the anatomy lesson. "You don't want me to run into someone, do you, Mr. MacCaster?"

"Oh my God, Evelyn," he said. "How in the name of Crucified Christ did you get us into this mess?"

Cars were careening along on both sides as though they had never been out of pasture before. It took the next ten minutes to get from the corner of Market up past the Brown Hotel. The traffic problem was really something about that time of day, God bless it. How I loved every hoggish, honking madman amongst them, especially truck drivers.

Mac was turning a dull green, slumped way over on his side of that gray upholstery, as though he was afraid someone would notice him. Which he was. Once or twice he got a grip on himself and sat up very commandingly.

"Get over so you can turn right here, honey."

But I just let a couple of dozen maniacs pretend they were better drivers than I was, which was a laugh—I could have turned around in the middle of the street if I'd had to—and he would simmer down again, groaning about the God-damn blank-blank traffic in this God-damn blank-blank town.

Then he slid over and put his arm across the back of the seat and began massaging my shoulder blades. To hell with the neighbors. "For Christ's sake, get out of this rat race, dear. We haven't got much time. Be a good kid. Pull over and let me drive."

I leaned against his hand a couple of times to keep him on the ball, and threw back my hair like Lana Turner. Then I managed to get pushed over into the left lane amongst all the cars taking the detour down past the wholesale houses along Commerce Street. That was really a madhouse because of the new construction for the overpass blocking up everything. We inched along over the cobblestones for blocks, with trucks and taxis and poor old wage earners trying to get home.

I chattered in a girlish way about how lovely the car was, but it didn't cheer him a bit. We finally got headed back toward the railway yards and the big clock on the station tower said four-fifteen. We had been enjoying the gasoline fumes and quiet uproar of downtown traffic for thirty minutes.

All at once he gave a look over his shoulder and then spun the wheel right out of my hands up a side street, and there we were coasting along in comparative peace and serenity.

It was just a last-minute rally though, and he knew it. The game was out of his hands. We were just around the corner from the Blue Bottle and time had fugited.

But he still had the old fighting spirit. He pulled the wheel right over into the curb so I had to stop. Quick as a flash he pressed that button and the old top came nipping down on us again, just a cozy nest for two.

Then he sat there looking at me.

"I like you, dear," he said, and you could have cut steaks with the edge on his voice. "But don't ever pull a stunt like that on your uncle again. You got what I like, Evelyn. But you didn't play fair with an old man, you know that, dear?"

He slid over so he had me pinned into the corner and the old devil reached right inside my jacket and yanked my shirt up and took a grip as though he intended to take half of me home with him.

I was so amazed I couldn't move, not to mention the fact that he was practically sitting on my lap. Then he went to work on the other side. He had a grip on me that Gorgeous George should know about. He was sort of gritting his teeth, too.

"*Stop* it, Mac."

"Pussy doesn't like?" He began to grin. "Well, dear, we know each other a *little* better now."

He slid over to his side and adjusted his jacket and felt his tie. If a baseball bat had been handy, even a nail file, *anything*, he wouldn't have looked so pleased.

"Old Mac wouldn't have played so rough if you hadn't cheated, dear." He was real friendly again. "Come on, hop to it, I got to get back to the grind. Oh, here—I don't go back on my word." He fished out his billfold and put a five-dollar bill in my pocket, the short-changing old bat.

"You're a liar!" I said. I was pretty steaming. It's no fun being grabbed by an old heel about ninety years old. "You said a ten."

That made him laugh like a loon. "You're okay, dear," he said. You would have thought we were bosom pals again, he sounded so tender. "You come on back soon. Use Mac halfway right and he'll use you *more* than right. Catch?"

"I don't like to play rough, dear. Feed old Mac the oats like a good sweet girl should and you don't even need a halter for the old horse. He's gentle as a baby. Come on now, let's see a smile on that pretty little face, so I can tell it's all patched up."

I pulled the Cadillac into his alley at thirty miles an hour and jammed on the brakes.

"Don't go 'way mad, dear. Look, I'm not. Who got the best of the bargain anyhow!" He was as genial as Santa Claus.

I ponied myself up to a weak smile. "Okay Mac. But you hurt me."

"Oh, listen, baby, don't *say* that."

He was out already, straightening his jacket and fluffing his trousers. "God, I wouldn't hurt a little girl like you for the world."

He came around and opened my door. "Look dear, here's the other five. Five for each of those handfuls you've got, and I'd give you a hundred if I ever thought old Mac harmed a hair of your head."

I debated whether to kick him where it would hurt the most, or let it go on the side of experience. After all, you never knew when a stinker like him would come in handy.

"Okay Mac," I said, with a misty smile. "We'll call it quits."

He gave me a pat on the shoulder, "Good girl!" and went galloping into the Blue Bottle as though a hornet was after him.

Hallelujah. Experience is a great teacher. And for ten dollars I could afford to give the old heathen a return engagement most any time.

Francis looked pretty sad sitting there in the shade of the Star Laundry and Cleaners, Press While You Wait, but they could have their Cadillacs. Was I glad to open his sprung old creaky door and fall in.

Susan bounced around to say hello, shuffling papers in her notebook, with her hair standing all which way from running her fingers through it. She looked all hepped up, hysterical from hunger, probably.

"I guess I took pretty long, Susie. Golly, you starved?"

"Starved?" she said as though the idea was absolutely startling. "No, I forgot all about being so hungry. Look, Evelyn, I wrote all this. It's long, about the seasons. Gosh, I've got to read it to you. I can't wait to hear how it sounds. The time just flew by."

"It did, huh?" I couldn't help being sarcastic, after all I'd been through. But she didn't even hear.

"Have a cigarette," she said, passing me that damn package of Kools. I never would have gotten it for her if I'd ever dreamed I'd be driven to the point of smoking them. "Now listen!"

"Don't you want to go—"

"No, first you've got to hear." She leaned back and took a deep breath, looking as though she'd just invented penicillin. "It makes you feel so . . . so sort of excited, Evelyn. I . . . I can't explain . . ."

She didn't have to tell me that. "Okay Sue, carry on!"

I couldn't decide whether to be exasperated or die laughing. But I had all those potato chips and beer holding me up, while all she had was a poem. It *was* long, though.

SEASONS
Spring comes with a whisper,
A freshet, a sigh. A cluster of robins,
Clouds scudding high.
The wind fails to chill,

Miriam Colwell

Only bully and bluster.
Tearing clothes from the line,
Even Father's great ulster.
But who minds the wind,
For it's spring.
The brown grass turns green,
Elms bear the sheen
Of new buds. The earth
Smells awake. Even you hesitate,
For back in the meadow,
There's one pussy willow.

A gray shift of fog,
And it's June.
Like a wraith gently bending,
A mantle descending. The skies disappear,
Here—a strange filigree.
My shrouded horizon becomes a webbed tree.
Then heat glances through,
And glazes the hill.
A bee slowly drones,
Holds me spellbound and still.
The shimmering sun
Lances out, strikes the bay,
Flashes here, sparkles *here*,
Like a witch, like a fey.
And through the long nights,
With stars crowding near,
The clear smell of clover.
Each light brings the hover
Of wings. Fragile things!

One short gaze must be all,
For it's Fall.

No brief color
Can shield what's in store,
No hoar-frosted lane
Hide the pain of decay,
As the red maple leaf
Bears my grief on the day
It lies trampled, and sore.

Oh, Season of Harvest,
Time fraught with dismay.
For in your lovely arms
Lies Winter's bleak mask. Hail
The outcast, most savage!
Then leafless the hedge,
The forest stands bare,
And once fertile lands
Bare the hands
Of cold sun.
Till, like a nun, comes the snow.
Drifting down,
In a city, a town,
A slow touch of magic.

So Winter,
So Spring,
Recurring, returning,
Ring of these Four.

  She finished all out of breath, and just sat there humped over her notebook, all the starch gone.
  "Holy smokes, it's good!" I said, trying to sound Oh, be joyful. When she was full of beans I could be exasperated, but the next

minute it was like trying to badger a turtle on its back. "Gee, I think it's fine, Sue."

"You really like it, Evelyn?"

"I sure do. Listen, let's go get something to eat, huh?"

I gave Francis a poke and he groaned like a bass fiddle. He always seemed to know when I had been fickle to him. Probably now he would cripple along for three days pretending to be sick, until I had to suck out his gas line.

"You don't really like it much," she said like a dying duck.

Dear loving God, these poets. You know, with no exaggeration, we could have sat there for two hours batting it back and forth: You did? You didn't . . . Well, what especially did you like? How about the line "fraught with dismay"? Yes, I certainly liked *that*. You mean you *really* liked that line, but does it seem a little too long? Oh, no, not a bit. Well, it's maybe a little shorter than . . . and so on. Endow me with patience, Saint.

Francis gave a lurch and decided he was alive.

"Look, I *like* it, Sue," I said, giving her arm a squeeze. "I wouldn't say so if I didn't, *would* I? You get nothing but the truth from me, kid. How about My Day? Don't you want to know what happened?"

All you needed was psychology, which in my opinion boils down to a little common sense. Everything had gone right out of her head while she was birthing this weather map, and now she got all upset for fear *my* feelings were hurt.

"Oh Evelyn, I'm such a stupe. What happened? Did he loan you some money? Golly, you were gone a long time."

"Yes, baby," I said. "And it's a long story which we'll save for another time. Only cast your eyes on this beautiful object."

I showed her just one of the fives, as she would have fainted to see them both. "What'll you have, caviar or hummingbirds' tongues? Let's go to the Lone Tree where they serve beer."

Part II

Afternoon

The Lone Tree had a long lunch bar down one side and very fancy booths. It had big mirrors and chromium fixtures and two-tone walls. The girls wore maroon and gray uniforms and caps to match, which they had to pay for themselves, but they could afford to as they made wonderful tips.

I knew a girl who worked there for a while. She was three years ahead of me in school, a junior when I was a freshman, and pretty dumb in a sort of inscrutable way, as well as very good-looking. Iris Wixon. I liked to pal around with Iris because while a lot of people might think she was the best looking, I could always keep three jumps ahead. Give or take a jerk I wouldn't want dead or alive.

After graduation she went up and got a job at the Lone Tree. Her hair got a lot blonder, and I guess she put every cent she made on her back. All the time she was in school she had a broken tooth, from falling out of a tree when she was a kid, but she could fix it up with wax so you'd never notice. Most of the time just at school she didn't bother, but when a dance or something came along, Iris could get herself up like a million, with her hair piled up high or some way, and a real, Believe me, I'm exotic look.

She only stayed up in town for a few months and the next thing I got a letter from her in Boston.

> Dear Evelyn,
>
> How's tricks back in the old corn patch? Here I am in Boston. Some fun. Why don't you come pay me a visit, Evelyn? I can show you a good time and don't mean maybe. Even get you a date, ha ha. I may start to train for a dental assistant. Anyhow am thinking about it as a fellow I know could get me a job. Right now I am still slinging hash but not complaining as making good money and three squares a day. You know my appetite. Ha ha.

Well, will close now. Drop a line and I mean it you coming up, Evelyn. We could tie one on in this town.

Keep your nose clean,
Iris

That summer she went out on Marblehead in a big summer hotel. And in the fall she and another waitress went down to Florida together to work, on the bus. I saw her once when she came home because her mother was sick, and she looked spectacular, believe me, a real dark suntan, and that hair, wearing a sundress without any top that made me drool.

She had it all figured, Marblehead summers and Palm Beach in the winter. Mrs. Rockefeller had nothing on her and she was all ready to wise the old man up to it if she ever saw him. On the way down that fall she and her friend were going to stop off a couple of weeks in New York City because they had met two guys who played in some night-club band.

"They're *spenders*, what I mean," she said. "All we do is go from one night spot to another. Nothing but the best! What a couple of clowns, oh my God! No kidding, Evelyn, I could get you a job so easy.

"You got it right though to finish school," she said. "A girl don't realize what an education means to her. Where are you nowadays without you don't graduate from high school, for Christ's sake? Every job they ask you. Well, let me know what's cooking in the old stewpot. God, nothing ever changes around here, does it?"

That was about two years ago and I hadn't seen her since, but whenever I saw her mother and had time to listen to all the things that ailed her, I asked about Iris and where she was.

The Lone Tree was pretty quiet at that time of afternoon, between hours, and a couple of the girls were sitting in the back having a cigarette.

For a while I had considered asking the manager for a summer job, but it was too close to home. I wanted to fly higher and see more. Then Charlie had been very waxy when I talked about it.

"My God!" he said, "you, a waitress. You'd wreck the place. They wouldn't have a customer left."

Which wasn't what he meant at all, but he got to it. "Jesus, Evelyn, Mother would really throw a cylinder."

We had a real rooting-tooting jamboree over that remark, and I was almost mad enough to work there just to twist the old girl's tail, but it didn't seem worth the effort. It was still in the backyard.

The hostess didn't wear a uniform. She had on a white blouse and pleated black skirt, and the welcoming smile she gave us congealed around the edges when she thought it over. We weren't getting any more stylish as the hours went by, but she should bother to snoot me, with *her* kisser, especially when I had money.

So I ignored her and picked out the booth we wanted and sat in it, while she was still waving her fanny down toward the back.

We ordered beer and fried oysters and hot pastrami on rye, and corn chowder to start, with french fries on the side. Also two packages of Chesterfields and one of Kools. I knew the waitress a little, and when the old hostess went switching by, I said, "Nature Girl wanted to stick us out in the kitchen someplace."

"That pain in the rear," she said. "Forget it, honey."

Susan made up an awful face at her first mouthful of beer. It was torture to watch her get through the first quarter of a glass, but after that her taste buds gave up the struggle and she got through the rest without visible pain.

I used to say, "Why bother, if it knocks you like that? No one's *making* you drink it, for the love of Mike."

But as I mentioned before, she wanted to be in on the battle, if it killed her. That is, some battles. You never could guess which one she would pick and which one she would pass up. That girl was an enigma to the general public, including me, even though most of the time we were best friends.

I put a quarter in the jukebox and we sat there feeling very calm and happy, having eaten the corn chowder and most of the french fries, and knowing more was on the way. All of a sudden it seemed as though the day had been pretty good, pleasanter than most, and that it was mainly because we were sitting in that particular booth together, drinking beer, and having Sue's notebook lying there beside the sugar bowl, and her hair all tousled from mental exertion—it didn't look at all bad that way, as a matter of fact—and her face all relaxed and happy and flushed, the way it got when she wasn't afraid someone was trying to push a grass roller over her, and the ten dollars in my pocket because I had outsmarted hot-pants MacCaster, Caddy and all, and with old Mrs. Puke Ogden still bellyaching about her oatmeal bread, no doubt, and what did we care anyhow? You're only alive once.

Susan could always tell pretty much how I was feeling, unless I didn't want her to, so we sat there listening to Sinatra singing "P.S. I Love You," grinning like Cheshire cats, at peace with the world.

Even Wiggling Fanny gave up trying to make icicles every time she went by, and actually stopped to ask if everything was all right, girls? I guess she was pretty decent underneath. Probably it was a tough job, being on her feet all day.

The hot pastrami was heavenly, and by the time the oysters came with more french fries and sliced tomatoes and cole slaw, we weren't so hungry but what we could settle down and enjoy everything. Including another bottle of beer to split.

But something always happens. There has to be a balance of forces or something, I guess. Of course things like that didn't bother me, variety being the spice of life, but with Susan it was like I meant about the grass roller.

These two kids from school happened to come in, the Waterfield sisters, and naturally when they saw us, they rushed right over to our table and sat down without pausing for breath.

Adele was short and squatty with round pop eyes, and believe me, she knew everything that happened, sometimes beforehand. Julia was a couple of years younger, and stupider, if possible, but she was a big horse already, and she certainly waved it around, thinking she was built like Lana Turner, which she wasn't. She had pimples that day, too.

Some doctor told me once if you have pimples on your chin it was from candy, and above your chin it was constipation. Candy must have constipated Julia.

"Look who's here!" Adele said, as though it was an original thought. "What *you* up to, hot shot? What's she up to, Susan? Who you gonna find to chew up and spit out tonight, huh?"

That was the way they were all the time, friendly but crude. Their natural habitat was the gutter.

Susan began to shrivel back into her shell like a periwinkle. That kind of chitchat made her very uneasy, which was why at school she was uneasy most of the time. Consequently when the kids didn't think she was a dope, they thought she was trying to be high-hat.

"If I know a good thing, would I spread it around?" I said. "How about a beer, girls, our treat?"

"You're *treating*!" Julia squealed. She looked a little like a pig too, with squinting little eyes, only I never saw a pimply pig. "God Almighty, Evelyn. You must of robbed a bank!"

As witty as a wet raincoat. To make conversation and also to keep them quiet, I told all about the movie, giving it a good build-up in hopes they might decide to go before the night prices went on, but not so.

Susan sat like a chicken with the pip, pretending to eat her dinner, and trying to act like she was amused when everyone else was. I could see Adele's eyes flitting around at her every so often, trying to think how she could stir the kid up. Especially after she had guzzled a glass of beer.

It wasn't that Adele was really mean, just that she never could pass anything out of the ordinary without poking it. I always intended leaving a hornet's nest in her path sometime.

Finally she had a brainstorm, and began to giggle like a lunatic. "Remember that time we went camping on the island, all us girls in the Senior play? That night when those guys from the construction crew tried to get in the boat with us to go over and have a big party? Oh my God! Susan got way up in the bow as far away as she could get. Those guys were really persistent, what I mean! Jesus, Susie, if you could of seen your face! I thought I'd wet my pants."

"Be more refined," I said, "for the love of Pete. You're in a public place."

"Whose fault is it they got functions?" She was really rolling now, with tears running down her face. Mrs. Milton Berle herself. "Listen, old Queen Victoria had to go. No different from you and me. You gotta go, you gotta go!"

Julia was right in there too, jiggling up and down and prodding me at every bounce.

"Stop it!" I said. "You're making me seasick. Go roll on the floor if you want to die laughing."

"Ev, oh Lord, my guts are aching. Remember that night you and Tud Evans and Charlie was in the hammock?"

"What was you *doing*? What you *mean*, they was in the *hammock*!" Julia fell on my shoulder and almost smothered me with her horrible combination of My Sin and Arrid. "What you *talking* about, anyways?"

"Listen to her! Ain't she the innocent!" Adele yelled. Those two should have been on the radio, Abbott and Horsetello. "What you *think*, stupid?"

I pushed Julia off and took a deep breath. There was still a half-plate of oysters left but this snappy dialogue was wearing me out. It was doing worse than that to Susan. She looked as though she was going to die any minute, and was afraid she wouldn't.

I wanted to give her a word of encouragement, something philosophical like it takes all kinds, but she wouldn't even look up. Anyhow, that was where Susan and I had a radical difference. Plenty of times I tried to show her there was no sense trying to beat her way upstream against the current, batting her brains out. My personal theory was, you might as well drift with the stream while you were in it.

"They're all part of the human race," I used to tell her. "Take a scientific attitude and maybe you'll find out something you didn't know."

But no, that wasn't for her. She had to keep at it the hard way.

"Look, you want to hear the prize about this kid sister of mine?" Adele was yammering. "Lemme tell you the prize about her and Ding-Dong!" Ding-Dong was Adele's steady and they were a perfect match.

Julia was squirming around on the table, as I refused to hold her up, listening with her mouth open and every pimple palpitating.

"What does she want but a *lesson!*"

"No kidding," I said. As a student of human nature, that struck me as very interesting. I mean, wasn't it? Truth is stranger than fiction all right, and a lot closer to home.

Anyhow, big mad joke. I laughed with them, mainly out of politeness.

Then Susan muttered that she had to go back to the Ladies, and stumbled out by Adele's knees with her head down so I couldn't see her face, but I didn't need to.

"God, she's a funny kid," Adele said, about the minute she'd gone. "What's she get outta life, anyhow? Huh?"

"Oh, the usual, I guess."

"The usual!" That panicked her. It didn't take much. "Where's she ever get it, for God's sake? Not from Edgar!"

"Can't you ever get your mind off sex?" I said coldly.

"What for, dear, what for?"

My facial muscles were aching from all this hilarity, and I was very tired of these cookies in general. Susan finally came back, looking as miserable as possible, and I hopped up and said, "Don't think it hasn't been . . . because it hasn't!"

As we walked out I muttered to Sue, "Leave 'em laughing, but for heaven's sake, leave 'em!" trying to cheer her up. But she really had a load of gloom.

It was about five-thirty. The street was full of mugs hurrying along home, and the sun was off the pavement, just hitting a few high windows.

It was sort of a lonesome time of day, with everyone looking worn-down and haggard, and hustling home to do all the things they should have done before they left for work, snapping at their wives or beating up the brats, or just sitting down to read the paper with their shoes off, wondering if it's worth the race or not.

Francis looked lonesome too, and old and tired. I gave him a pat. "We all got to go sometime, dear."

For a while we just sat. I felt a little dumpy too. I had that Where do we go from here feeling again. But it never lasted too long with me. Pretty soon that old joy de vive began to set in. What was so awful, after all, we had just eaten, but well, and still had money to burn. The night was ahead, and who's to say how the wheel may spin?

"Let's go see another movie, Sue. Want to? Or do you want to go home?"

Poor kid. She wanted to go home right then the way she wanted a hole in the head. To face Mrs. Becker and old Livewire asking where she had been and why, and Mrs. Becker worried about the company she was keeping, me, and worried when she went off by herself without me, and going to be worse than worried if she ever suspected that Hine Hanscomb, a married man, was nosing around. But it wasn't so much on account of that, the worrying, that Susan minded going home right then. It was because she was all stirred up like soup inside, and feeling about as gay as Francis looked, and when you're in a state like that, you don't want somebody old, and too close in your own family, no matter how much you love them or vice versa, needling and fussing and worrying themselves sick over what ails you. When you don't know yourself, which is the whole trouble.

"Know what you can do?" I said. "You can call up the barbershop and tell your uncle where you are and that you are going to the movies, and won't be home until later. So they won't worry.

Miriam Colwell

And get him to call Ma and tell her. That way we save phone calls."

Also that way I wouldn't have to talk to my mother, who would certainly have blistered the wires.

'Tell him to tell Ma I haven't forgotten about the orders," I said. Then all of a sudden the place in my throat where my conscience appears to live began to sting like fury. I thought of my mother and what a mess I'd left her with—all that bread sitting around—and how she didn't even know where I was. Maybe you haven't realized how much I love my mother, but anybody who knows her would *know*. There isn't a soul in the whole town that doesn't love my mother. She may not be a ball of fire but, believe me, I wouldn't exchange her for two and a half million dollars and I mean it.

"Listen," I said, trying to stop thinking what a lousy trick I'd pulled, "ask him if Jonas is there and get him to go deliver those orders for Ma and I'll pay him tomorrow. No, wait, I'll call Mr. Becker myself."

I went into the drugstore and got through to Mr. Becker, which cost me sixty cents. I straightened Susan out with him and finally got it through his lightning brain that I wanted Jonas, whereupon he laid down the receiver and yelled "Jonas," which lifted a great weight off my mind.

Of course Hell on Wheels Kerr had to make bright chat to the tune of another sixty cents before he said, sure, he'd go right over and deliver the orders if my mother would give him a piece of graham-cracker pie. That was out of my hands. But my mother would give anything to most anybody, especially male, with Jonas's gab, so everything was under control.

To give Francis a little exercise we drove out Union Street, instead of straight across town to the Royal. On the corner of Union and Bank was the bakery Charlie and I had stung for a phony ad.

It made me sort of wistful to remember the afternoon we went in there together. After all, Charlie represented two years out of my life, and he was a peachy dancer. Also pretty cute in his bulldog sort of way. I really loved the stinker in my own fashion, and probably would never quite forget him.

Then I cheered up thinking how nuts he was about me, probably trudging down some hotel corridor right this minute with a trunk under his arm, yearning to know what I was doing and when he was going to get home for a date.

So much for nostalgia. It's strictly for the poetic type.

Some kids were playing baseball in the park between Union and Fern, and a few people were sitting around on the benches under the elms. It looked very soothing to the spirit out across the park, the green grass like velvet, and the blossoming hydrangea bushes, and the tall old trees with little round beds of flowers around their trunks, all lying there in the red sunlight, which didn't reach as far as Fern Street anymore, so I parked for a while. The kids were shouting but it was far enough away to sound pleasant, and occasionally you could hear the cars down on the Avenue at the traffic light.

A little yellow and black Drake's Cakes truck kept hopping from house to house on North Park. I could see the driver go tearing up to a door, and back to the truck, and back to the door, probably an hour or so late because he had stopped to watch a ball game on television.

His wife and kids would really catch it when he got home after that workout, tired and grouchy. If she had any sense she'd have a bottle of beer for him in the refrigerator. But instead, ten to one, she would light into him before he got the screen door open, "Where you *been*? Your supper's cold, the kids couldn't wait, and I was planning to go next door to watch TV, so 'course you had to be late tonight, of all times to be late." And he would say, "So what, for Christ's sake? I should race my tail off so you can watch the Lone Ranger?" and they would finally work up a real entertainment for the neighbors.

I could sit and amuse myself like that quite a while if I had nothing better to do, but Susan needed my attention. Sometimes it was quite a strain to have to be normal for both of us.

"Cheer up, dear," I said. "Why let those two goons spoil our perfectly good day?"

I didn't call anyone "dear" often. So she knew I was really concerned and it warmed her cold little heart to the core. That was one trouble with me. I could see through people too easy. Which was why every once in a while I got tired of looking at the same old views.

"They just make me sick," she said, very low. "Why can't I be like you, Evelyn, and just laugh it off? I can't. It . . . it just makes me want to crawl off out of sight, where I can take a bath and change all my clothes . . . only . . . only that won't make me feel clean again. It's as though . . . as though they've left their dirty old stupid talk on me like . . . like dirty fingerprints, and I can't get rid of them."

She gave a real shiver, as though she was having a chill. I had never seen her quite so stirred up on the outside. Mostly she kept it inside until she got out of sight, and then I guess she kept it on the inside too. "Sometimes I think if I ever have to look at them again, I'll . . . I'll just go crazy—honest, I mean it. They're so . . . dis*gust*ing."

"Oh listen, Sue, they're harmless. Just a little on the moron side. They mean all right."

"They don't mean *any*thing, anything at all, but cheap sexy trash. That's all they know. You think they even know there's more to the world than that? They don't. They don't! They never will."

She was almost crying, but I think she would have jumped out of the car and walked the fifty miles home before she would let me see her give up and shed a tear. Maybe you have to be bottled up like that before you can write poems and stuff, but, brother, deliver me. A good cry, especially when you're with someone who gives a darn, is like a laxative, it does you a world of good. Once in a while, I mean. Too much is too much of anything.

"Look honey," I said, to calm her down or work her up or something, "don't let a couple of easy Annies like them throw you. But you know, dear, honest, you got to stop being so scared of sex. There's a lot in it, believe me."

There we were, sitting beside the park, watching the grass and trees grabbing at the sunlight as though they weren't going to let go, and a very peaceful feeling of the kids running off one and two at a time, for supper, until there was only a pitcher and a batter left, and everything very quiet in the neighborhood except for a jet way up overhead, and Susan and I all of a sudden having this very serious conversation.

"You just take advice from your aunt Evelyn," I said, in a very motherly tone, and I certainly felt about thirty years older than she was, regarding what we were talking about. "Honest, Sue, you got to give it a chance, and stop being so finicky. Look, you can't fool around with Edgar much longer, I mean, he's all right, God knows, I *like* Edgar, but he couldn't excite a grasshopper, what I mean.

"I know you hate to have me talk like this and it's none of my business, maybe, and all that baloney, but, gosh, we're pretty close to each other, Sue, we're as close as sisters, and I can't see you getting all worked up without it hurts me too. Honest, I mean, it's so silly. Now the whole thing is, you've listened to a lot of these dumb dopes and you've been milling it around inside you for years. My God, the stuff you hear down there at school would make your hair curl if you wanted to be sensitive about it. The trouble is, you're so darned shy, even with *me*. I mean, *me!*"

She wouldn't look over, so I pulled her face around. You'd have thought I had been laying her vital organs out one by one for the passersby to gawk at. When you came right down to it, I guess she didn't trust me, even if she did like me more than anyone else, because the way she looked at it, I was very palsy with most everyone—not just her—jokers and jellyfish included. I didn't really blame her. In fact, sometimes, I had to admit, she showed pretty good judgment.

She couldn't help smiling a little around the edges, so I gave her a poke and said, "Light me a fag, for God's sake, this soul-searching is activating my saliva."

Which she did, and we were back on solid ground. In fact, she didn't want to stop talking about it. Like eating sour pickles. You don't really like the taste but it's tantalizing.

Way up in the sky the jet looked like a streak of fire with the sun on it.

"I don't know, maybe I'm . . . maybe I'm crazy or something," she said, "but I couldn't . . . I mean . . . I couldn't go with Joe, Evelyn. Truly, I couldn't. On the picnic that time, you remember last year, I just had to . . . to go behind the bushes and . . . and I was sick. Everybody was paired off under a blanket or something and I couldn't get away from him and, and his . . . his wet old mouth just made me sick at my stomach and he kept . . . kept trying to . . ."

She was all upset again, hardly able to keep her lips from quivering.

"That slob." I was a little upset myself, thinking of how it must have been. He was a real fat ass and I should have had more sense. I guess, to tell the truth, I was probably too occupied at the time to care much.

"And . . . and that trumpet player, Eddie, that you brought by that time, you and Charlie."

"I remember."

I remembered all right. "What gives with your girlfriend?" he said, next time I saw him. "Maybe she don't like musicians. Look, Evelyn, I'm too old to play paper dolls. I don't take a girl out, even on a double date with you, baby, to talk about what's socialism or some God-damn tripe. Tell her when she wants to warm up, to send me a carrier pigeon, and I'm her boy. She wouldn't even take a drink of gin, for Christ's sake. What was she afraid, I had the hoof and mouth?"

"Is something the *matter* with me?" Sue said now. She didn't sound as though she really thought so—more as though the world was wrong. "Is there anything wrong with me, Evelyn? I couldn't stand it. I couldn't stand it. I couldn't stand it to have Eddie touching me. My . . . my body is private, it's . . . it's me, and I couldn't stand him . . . stand him . . . you know . . . trying to feel under my sweater. It's . . . it's not like an old coat I could take off and throw away after a lot of ninnies went feeling it all over. It's a part I can't get away from—like the things I think and the things I feel that . . . that I couldn't tell anyone if I had to die. After Joe that night I wanted to die—I couldn't wash his taste out of my mouth—I couldn't wash the way I felt off, and it was awful for days. I hated myself. I couldn't stand the thought of having him know part of *me* when I didn't like him, even; when I can't bear the way he wears his pants as though they're going to fall off and the way he slouches around and grins.

"And Eddie was just as bad. He was worse. He didn't even want to talk at all . . . to even get acquainted. I never met him till that night. How did he think I wanted to . . . to do things like that—with someone I hadn't even had a chance to see really what they looked like? How could I even know if I *liked* him or not? When I only saw him under the light for about two minutes and after that just in the dark. Maybe dogs and cats act like that—maybe just anyone, any other dog and cat is all the same to them—but it ought to be different with people. Hadn't it? Would you just have let him go on kissing and all that as though you were crazy about him when you didn't even know if he was tall or . . . or bow-legged or blue-eyed or cross-eyed or . . . or . . ."

She was almost laughing now. It was pretty remarkable the way she could sometimes change her state of mind in no time flat.

"Would you, Evelyn?"

I guess she caught me with my conscience showing, because my face began to feel hot. I couldn't say no because maybe I'd done just that on occasion, and it hadn't seemed bad at the time, but looking at it through her eyes it could seem pretty savage. The way I felt about such things, everyone was entitled to their own opinion—win, lose or draw.

"Okay," I said, leaning out the window, pretending to watch a crazy kid roller-skating way down on South Parkview, "so you drew a couple of lulus. But that doesn't mean you should give up the game, Susie. And if you don't circulate you won't ever meet up with the right guy. Maybe in the movies he always happens to pick her up when she falls on her fanny skating or something, but it don't happen so easy in real life, baby. You got to be right out beside the main highway to get the good hitches. I'm telling you. And then you got to be friendly, Susie. I mean, you're intellectual and all that, but most people haven't got a brain to bless themselves with and they don't want to be reminded. Look, I'm telling you for your own good. I know, strictly from the old try-anything-once school. That way you learn fast."

"You think there's something wrong with me, Evvie?" She didn't sound very upset. In fact, she wasn't really asking a question. It was more as though she was teasing me.

Yesterday she would have curled up and died before she would have come out with something like that. When I came to consider it, the whole conversation was pretty unusual for her.

Then came the dawn. Evelyn saw the light. All this time what she had really had on her mind was Hine Hanscomb, probably all day, carrying him around with her like a charm piece. That sad-eyed jerk. He had really gotten his foot in the door and believe me, she wasn't making it hard. He had passed inspection and the kid was all of a sudden on the inside looking out.

For some reason it got under my skin, and she knew it right away.

"What's so special out the window?" She was so cocky, you could have shot her off like a gun. "You think there's anything the matter with me, Evvie, for feeling that way, about Joe and Eddie, I mean?"

"Oh Christ, no, you're just queer." I felt cross and I guess I looked cross, because she didn't say a word while Francis and I grunted and groaned and finally got going.

I was tired of that old park and all the birds tweeting away and the sun in my eyes. We turned around by Hood's Ice Cream and headed back across town. Francis felt jumpy too, and coughed and jerked and shook as though he was coming down with double pneumonia. Probably that crumb bum at the filling station watered his gas.

When we stopped at the red light by Sears and Roebuck, I looked to see if she was down in the dumps again, but she gave me a quick smile, with her eyes crinkling the way they did when she felt good.

"I'm glad we're not going home yet. It'll be dark when we get out of the movie, Ev. We've had fun today, haven't we?"

I guess I have a lousy disposition, but I couldn't snap out of it the way she did. "Sure we have," I said, "but . . ."

"But what, Ev?"

"Oh, I've got this feeling, that's all. I know it's crazy. I only have one once in a while but then I *know*. You'll think I'm nuts, but I've got this feeling that he's not right for you, Susie."

I was too busy maneuvering Francis backwards and uphill into a parking space to see her reaction, but I was amazed at the way she yanked down her sweater, and of all things, fished my comb out of Charlie's pocket. Talk about lightning personality changes. Brother!

Then she hopped out on the pavement. "Who's arguing?" She was so chipper that I lost my grouch on the spot and we sailed up the hill into the Royal giggling like fools.

That movie was something else on your tintype-Bible times. On one of those wide screens that fracture your eyes. Half the screen is fuzzy and the other half is Victor Mature with a stomachache. He had indigestion all through it. I finally began to pity the poor lion that was going to be forced to eat him. No telling what horrible effect it would have on the beast. Cancer of the pancreas, ulcers, anything.

Naturally there was a lot of horsing around with swords, and trying to decide who had the spirit and who didn't, but it wasn't too bad. I've seen worse.

It was almost eight when we came out on the street again. All the lights were on down State, though it wasn't really dark. It wasn't really dark but it wasn't day anymore, and the whole feeling of the world was different, a nighttime feeling.

Heels sound different at night, they loiter more, and when you look at someone they're looking right back at you, maybe laughing, maybe What the hell, maybe Hel*lo*, baby. And the cars are quieter, even Francis, which is saying a mouthful.

Even a bus is something pretty different at night when it goes by and you get a glimpse of a real cool blond boy peering out in a gabardine raincoat, or a Negro woman with a couple of cute little Negro kids. It always reminded me of a movie just at dark like that, especially when I just came out of one, and everything I did, walking out on the street and looking at my reflection in a window, the things I said, the way I laughed, and lighted a cigarette, or stared at a crummy-looking dame, it all seemed to be a scene I was going through, a casual sort of street scene, but with a tenseness underneath because something was just on the point of happening. A gunshot, Alan Ladd running up the pavement with blood on his hands, or a couple of ordinary-looking jokers coming out of the Brass Tongs across the street getting into a blue Olds, with the cops watching them through the plate glass right behind my reflection.

Which was pretty funny, until I straightened my pedal-pushers and opened my jacket so I could show out through. Right away a couple of Air Force men came up behind us and began to whistle.

What a scrubby pair they were, though. One had a neck like a picked chicken, and the other one had boils. That faded-out Air Force blue made them look as though they had shrunk with their clothes on, pre-shrunk man, guaranteed washable and tub-fast.

There was very little color to worry about with these cucumbers. Susan gave them one look and started for Francis at a gallop. So it came to nothing. Anyhow I was too tired to parley-vous with strangers.

We were both shot. Once we had flopped in the front seat neither of us had the energy to make a move. The General Electric neon sign kept flashing across Susan's face so that she looked like part of *An American in Paris*, where all the dancers are going berserk, dancing, and the lights are flashing all colors over everything—or that was as I remembered it. Gene Kelly and Leslie Caron were all right dancing down on the Seine, but all that whoopdedoo later seemed to go on forever.

Anyway, from the time he was stupid enough to pick Leslie Caron instead of the other one who really had something, as well as money, I lost interest in the whole thing. How dumb can you get? It was the same way with Fred Astaire.

Charlie used to drag me to every Astaire movie that ever was, and it was murder. I mean, he's a wonderful dancer and all that, but why should I sit still all evening to look at a face like that? And pay money for it into the bargain. I do it all day long for nothing. There's nothing wrong with my imagination that I can see, but it was certainly a strain on it to watch those dames always end up by falling for him. Except that movie he did with Rita Hayworth. That I could believe. They made a lovely couple in a horrible way.

Brother, I never saw such long legs. It made me very nervous for fear she would make a mistake and step on him, which would have been good-bye Mr. Astaire, good-bye. Charlie got in a real sweat that night. He kept hissing, "Shut up, God damn it, shut up, lame brain. What did I bring you for? Jesus, I'm nuts." All the time so stirred up playing handsies that he couldn't sit still, until an usher came by and warned him to be quiet.

He loved the Marx Brothers too. Whenever the Royal ran one of those old has-beens, we had to drive clear to town after school to see it.

I used to thank God for Allen Jones who was a relief to look at for a little minute while he sang a song. Men who smoke cigars all the time never interested me. There's something really nauseating to watch a man roll a cigar around in his mouth. I mean, it looks lewd, like going to bed in front of the Fuller Brush man or someone.

"You pooped, Susie?" I said. "Light me a butt, like a good girl."

We both had that God damn it, nothing to do now but go home feeling.

Francis was sitting way back on his can, the side street was so steep. I usually parked on that street because up at the top where it intersected with Broadway, there was a big old church built right into the hill. It was Greek or something, and had a funny look that I liked. Until the last minute, driving toward it, it looked as though you were going to drive right in. I never noticed churches much, any more than houses.

There were two at home, one little one, which the Baptists built out of spite, and the big old one that was built God knows how long ago and supposed to be for anybody that wanted it, whatever religion they were. Nobody used it anymore except for a funeral when they expected a big turnout, and once every summer when Reverend Ogden preached there.

When I was real little I could remember a steeplejack way up in a sling painting the top of the steeple, which had mostly worn off by now. I once heard old lady O. going on a great rig about how beautiful it was and its lovely lines and its lovely pews and what a shame it was to use that atrociously ugly, stubby little Baptist church instead. She was always stirred up about something like that. I couldn't see that it was worth raising your blood pressure about; they were both churches, one bigger than the other.

But this one on the hill behind the Royal struck my fancy, maybe because it was practically necking with the back of a movie house. In some queer way it had something to do with the way I felt in a city, more alive or alert or expectant or something. Here was this odd-looking duck of a church out of Turkey or someplace, right there smack on Broadway, with a candy store on one side, and a graveyard on the other, with Liggetts Drugs handy on the corner. It's hard to explain what I mean when I don't know myself.

Susan looked sleepy, holding her knees against the dashboard to keep from sliding off the seat. Her eyebrows were drawn together—they were one of her best features, sleek and black with a keen natural line, just perfect. I never could get mine quite the same, though I tried often enough, and sometimes got so disgusted that I yanked them all out and used a pencil. Charlie had fits about that, mostly on his mother's account. She told him to try to hint gently that it looked cheap, like a carnival girl. I didn't let one grow for months after that remark.

I took a big stretch and yawned, letting the steering wheel hold me up, and started to say Oh shit, we might as well go home. But caught it back in time.

If there was one thing that got Susan's goat it was that word. I think it was the worst thing, bar none, anybody could say to her. She never forgot if a person happened to use it, either. The way when some kid made a real assy fool of himself, you didn't want anyone to see you with such a dumbhead.

It was one subject I never argued with her about, because she just couldn't see reason. Anyway, why bother; there were plenty of other words in my vocabulary.

I guess it all went back to one time when she was real small, five or so, and she was playing around waiting to go home from the barbershop with Uncle Wildfire. When she was little she wore her hair cut straight across in bangs, same as now, and even I can remember those big old black eyes of hers staring out at the world as though she was never quite sure what was going to happen next.

This Joe Palooka, an old farmer from some old shack back in the woods, was having his hair cut, and I can imagine the scintillating conversation he and Uncle Becker must have chewed back and forth. Anyhow, finally old Becker finished and waved the hair off the apron all over the floor—at least he always does—and stuffed the quarter in his pocket, and probably had to sit down to recuperate from fifteen whole minutes on his feet.

Old Joe Palooka came shuffling out past Susan who was minding her own business on the doorstep, and said, "Hey, sis, what's that dirt on your face there? A piece of shit?" chuckling away as though he was getting off a droll bit of humor.

Susan has never forgotten him, either. I bet she could describe him today as plain as Eisenhower. In fact, she described him so plain to me that I saw him walking down Maple Street one day and I could have gone right up and batted the old fool in his big mouth. Except I had to admit he looked pretty old and pathetic. He had dirty old mustaches drooping around his mouth, which was droopy too and covered with tobacco juice, and he hadn't shaved for a month. One of his Old Ironsides suspenders was broken and his pants were sagging, and if they had ever fitted he had lost about fifty pounds. Altogether, knowing his history and all, it gave me the wilby-golgies.

Anyway, she tried to explain to me what an awful feeling she had—maybe she did have that on her cheek. A grown-up man ought to know, and I guess she almost passed out from such a horrible thought.

There was the difference between us right there. If it had been me, I'd have swiped the dirt off and probably spit at the old goat for his nasty mind, but you know what she did? She ran and hid behind the poolroom in an old ramshackle shed Becker kept coal in, and they didn't find her until nine o'clock that night, with the whole town out hunting, and all that time she hadn't dared to wipe at her cheek for fear it *was* there, and she couldn't bear to touch it. So the poor little dumb cluck was almost going crazy.

That was Susan for you.

"Well, Susie," I said, "no place to go but home, I guess."
"Okay by me."
When we turned left by the church I could look right in and see people facing the altar and a lot of lighted candles.
"We ought to go take a peek in there, sometime, Susie, you know it?"
"Sure," she said, waking right up. "That would be fun."

She was always ready to do something wacky like that, but I wasn't in the mood. My spirits were flagging. Here it was going on nine o'clock of a summer evening, just when things were really beginning, and we had nothing to do but go home. For God's sakes, it was depressing. It made me feel like a wallflower or something. Even those two blokes from the airfield would have been better than nothing, a base of operations, you might say, but I could never have sold them to Susan.

I began to feel a little disgusted with her for being such a goop. This happened once in a while, and sometimes she saw it coming and got ready to duck, and sometimes just wandered off with her feelings hurt.

But tonight she just sat there humming "P.S. I Love You," not giving a darn. We were going along Front Street past a lot of closed stores and a warehouse plastered with circus posters and a little hole-in-the-wall beer joint, and for a minute I played with the idea of parking there and letting a couple of guys pick us up just to give her a turn. But I let it pass, as too wearing, even on me; then it would have really made her sore. At the traffic light, a Buick convertible came up beside us, purring like the world was its oyster. It's a funny thing, but you rarely see the convertible type in a convertible. This chum had a crew cut on a real egg head, no neck to speak of, and glasses, plus large ears. His date was dead set to enjoy herself, but it was going to be work from the word go.

He was resting his arm nonchalantly on the door, discoursing, probably on something like the amount of water displaced by a foot of solids, I could picture him letting himself go in a chemistry laboratory.

She was listening with that intense expression that meant she was bored to tears, but after all, it was a balmy summer night and he did have a nifty car. I didn't waste a minute's pity on her. In fact, I sat there giving them a cold stare, and savoring every miserable everlasting moment that evening was going to be for her.

At her age she should know it's not what you do, it's who you do it with that counts. Though a lot of people never get something simple like that through their heads, from the cradle to the grave. I guess I was just born knowing some things, and some others I picked up from my mother. She must have been quite a girl in her day. Poor Ma, she had a fallen womb and no wonder, the way she tore around waiting on my father and me. That was why I had to pay back the money she borrowed from the Credit Union, and *quick*. So she couldn't keep saying she didn't go to the doctor because it cost too much.

When the light turned, the Buick left Francis as though he was crippled, which wasn't too wrong, and went off up Main Street flitting its tail around another car like a jet playing with a windmill. If I hadn't got a good look at those two, my blood would have curdled with envy.

But how often do you see someone who just exactly fits? The minute they parked the car somewhere and got out for a beer, he would turn into a funny-looking guy who was self-conscious about being shorter than his girlfriend and tried to cover up, being the analytical type, by gabbing every minute and hanging right at her elbow to show he couldn't care less. While she was going to wear herself out being bright and witty, going back in her mind to what she'd said a minute ago to see if it sounded stupid, and going forward beyond what he was saying to what he *might* say, to which she could bring out something really super— in short, paying very little attention to him at all, being all taken up with herself.

I guess I felt a little sour about convertibles. It was an elegant evening. Cool but not cold, and the bridges upriver looked like Christmas decorations. It was always around this time of night that I began to start perking. Maybe I was born to be a chorus girl. Except that the same old grind night after night would leave me cold. Variety was my motto.

Susan was mumbling along, humming half under her breath, and I picked up the words and began giving them a real treatment: "P.S. I love you. . . ."

When I really felt like it I sounded as good as anyone on the radio. So for a while Kay Starr and Eartha Kitt had to make way.

The radio towers on outer School Street were winking and blinking, with stars beginning to show above them. Francis began to feel a lot better and forgot about three-quarters of his ailments. Cars were pulling off into the right lane for the outdoor movie, and Susan stared up at the billboard with a half-willing look, but my fanny had taken enough punishment for one day. Anyhow, it was just because she dreaded going home, not because she craved to see *Frankenstein Meets Hopalong Cassidy* or something.

I began to start simmering all over again. She didn't want to go home but she didn't want to pick up a couple of guys to fool around with. What in God's name did she want to do? Just put off the question by going to another movie. Evading the issue. She was a great little evader of vital issues. Where did she think she was headed, being so childish and all? My God, she had to start facing the facts of life, and the night was made for love. Which I began to sing, making like Judy Garland. Really dying for someone in my mind's eye, miles away from a peculiar, finicky, flighty, big-brain, black-headed female who happened to be tagging me around.

The cars went whooshing by, making Francis tremble as though we were in a wind tunnel. There was still a streak of color along the horizon. From the tops of the hills you could see patches of farmland with corn partway up, and borders of trees between the fields.

Susan sat with her knees hunched up, looking out, not saying a word. To tell the truth, she looked miles away too, God knows where, but she was taking it big. Then all of a sudden she started to laugh.

"What's so funny?"

"Oh nothing," she said, in a sort of remote way. "Just something I was thinking."

Then she hauled back into herself, and I might as well have been driving the Alaska Highway with an unconscious deaf-mute for company.

I began to feel slightly put upon. Whose car was it anyhow, and who had gotten the dough to splurge around with all day? She had been just as ready to eat and just as ready to go to the movies, but had she lifted a hand? All she'd lifted a hand to do was write a poem. That hadn't fried any oysters, or bought any tickets. Not that I expected her to turn inside out with gratitude or anything, but this soaring away in the clouds business struck me as being very poor manners.

"How about going down to Lily's for a game of bridge?" I said.

Lily was an old buddy of mine, though I can't remember how it happened. She was about forty-five and lived on the Town Dump Road, and every time she opened her mouth I had to laugh. Her complexion was red—reddish hair, reddish eyebrows, and reddish freckles on the backs of her hands. She always kept her eyebrows plucked way up so that her expression was one of strained surprise, sort of, on top, and deadpan underneath, with a cigarette always hanging in her mouth which she talked around. The most typical way I think of her is sitting across the card table, with her head pulled back to keep smoke out of her eyes, a lungful dribbling over her chin, her eyebrows up under her hair someplace, and a real sly old glint in her eye. The reason she liked me was because she knew I didn't give a damn. It would tickle her to death to hear about getting the three bucks out of Crazy Swazy. "My God, you kids," she would say, "what'll you think of next? Pour me out some beer, that's a girl, my corns are aching."

Then she would sit there with her legs spraddled out and her slippers falling off and laugh and cough and stamp out butts, with her little reddish eyes going over my face like a vacuum cleaner.

Lily had a bad reputation, which was why I had a good time going there. As long as I ever knew her, she'd been living with a married man who was still supposed to be living with his wife. Not that he ever would strike you as a Romeo. He looked more like a sheepdog, with those woebegone pouchy eyes, but they were satisfied.

She was no Juliet, either. That would have put her in hysterics. "God Almighty," I can hear her say, spitting beer, "Brick and me? Shakespeare? What you want for fifty cents, kid, anyway? Five dollars' worth of bull?" She loved her own jokes.

I used to go around to her house every couple of weeks or so, and sometimes we would play bridge if there was anyone around, or just sit and hash things over.

She didn't take to Charlie at all. I took him there one night, and he was all set to sit around in a scarlet woman's boudoir as though he did it all the time, Joe College stuff which he was sometimes full of. Next time I saw her, on the street in front of Tucker's store, she said, "For Christ's sake, leave your tittie baby to home after this, kid. I can turn on the radio if I want to hear corny jokes. You got him where he don't know which end is up, but it don't interest me."

Then she was afraid my feelings were hurt so she pinched my arm and swallowed half a Chesterfield and said, "I'm just an ugly old son of a biscuit, dear. But I can't change my nature now. When you coming over to have a rubber? Brick'll be around the end of the week, and maybe we can scrape up a foursome."

I always wondered what kind of perfume she used. It had a sort of hard sour-spice, tantalizing, but prickly smell, and it seemed as much her as her skin. She always smelled of it, whether she was slopping around doing a week's dishes or dressed for town, but I could never find it anywhere, in her bedroom or in the bathroom, and she just laughed when I asked. "Want me to leave it to you in my will, kid? Judas, they say curiosity killed the cat."

Susan went there with me a few times because she liked to play bridge, but she was always pretty uneasy, like a kid that wants to watch the puppet show but wishes he wasn't quite so close. Lily's living room was pretty small, and once we got the card table up and everyone smoking like chimneys, it got smaller and smaller, so you began to feel like you were sitting in each other's lap. Which might happen after a little lubrication. Brick was affectionate like a sheepdog too. Susan's eyes always got bloodshot from a lot of smoke, and she got paler and paler after two glasses of beer, while everyone else got redder and redder. But Brick liked her for some strange reason. He always asked about her, and he teased her just like he did me, about going to the john often, or being skinny, or having big feet—anything. The funny thing was, she never minded, just grinned at him and looked sort of flustered, but not all upset the way she would have from anyone else.

Brick was impressed with her being salutatorian of our class, and he got as mad as a hatter when I told him she should have had top honor because her rank was really higher than Charlie's.

"Why, the damned dirty bastards," he shouted. "What they trying to pull? That nice little girl, she's got the stuff, and those sons of bitches fouling her up. By God, I got a good mind to . . . to . . ."

Lily just listened to him with her head thrown back and one eye squinted, shuffling the cards.

"By God, I'd like to . . . why, you know that kid is smart? She's got brains, you can tell that by looking at her. Those crooked G.D. monkeys."

"The woman always gets the short end," Lily said, narrowing her eyes at him across the table. "Ain't you ever heard that, Brick? Come on now, play your hand. You wasn't cut out for no reformer."

Brick had diabetes and liver trouble both, and sometimes the old pouches under his eyes were really rugged. He gave himself a shot of insulin every day on the dot as regular as a clock, and once he showed me his leg all covered with pricks like a pincushion.

"I been in and out of the hospital so almighty often," he said, "the last time I told them damned if I was going home. I said I'm going to go pitch me a tent out front in the parking lot where I'll be handy."

Lily never told me whether she liked Susan or not, but she always seemed glad to see her, and that old girl never bothered to pretend feeling what she didn't.

Late in the evening I would sometimes notice Lily sitting there with her cards in front of her, watching Susan over her cigarette smoke like an old sphinx. But the only thing she ever said was, "A smart cookie, huh? God, she doesn't have much to say, does she? Some different from you, kid! You can do enough gabbing for the both of you, huh? Who's her feller? Who takes her round?"

"Ed Preble."

"Oh, zat so?" she said, and that ended the subject. "Get me some more beer, Evelyn, my corns are aching."

"How about going down to Lily's?" I said again. She looked up as though I had startled her out of a coma, her eyes real dark and warm, and ready to head for the woods at a moment's notice.

"Lily's? My God, there's nothing I'd rather do less."

If I hadn't had Francis on my hands I might have fainted from sheer shock. Nothing she'd rather do less. Well fancy that. Added to which she had taken the name of the Lord in vain. The times Susan could bring herself to swear I could count on about one finger. She was really building up steam. Because I knew how she felt about religion and God and so on—we had talked about it plenty of times. She claimed she was an agnostic, which I looked up every so often when I wanted an excuse to leave the room and use the library at school. There was always someone in there you could fool around with and sometimes even sneak a cigarette. But I never got what *agnostic* meant through my head. That and *atheist*. One was worse than the other, but it was always a stab in the dark which was which.

Susan and Mr. Shaw, the principal, had quite a ball throwing them back and forth in English Lit class one day, while the rest of us sat there with our mouths open, because she was about the quietest one usually. It was all about a book, *The Way of Flesh* or something, which I always meant to read out of curiosity.

But Susan had thought about stuff like that quite a lot. She had the time. She didn't believe in God, like anyone sitting on a throne in heaven watching every move us poor suckers made on the earth, but she could never get very definite about what she did think He was.

I went with her to the Public Library one Saturday. The Library down home was in back of Tucker's store, a dinky little building built sideways, open once a week, when she was after some book explaining the Bible. To the common reader. Charlie's Aunt Maude was librarian and had been since the flood, and when Sue asked for this book, she almost split a whalebone.

"I'm sure I don't understand Miss Chase"—as though it would have made a big difference if she'd just been consulted—"a lot of people are going to be very misled, *very* misled, girls, by her book. I'm sure, you understand, that Miss Mary Ellen Chase is a good Christian woman, but she has done herself an injustice, trying to tear the Bible down and belittle it. *No* one expected, after all her books that I've read and *enjoyed*, to find a lack of sanctity in her attitude towards the Greatest Book on Earth. For one, I know I can *never* feel the same about what she writes again.

"It's the holiness we expected; I'm sure we all expected holiness and Holy Reverence. That's what we ought to be made to feel when we touch the Holy Book. I'm sure I *don't* know what she's driving at, girls, but the way I feel myself, I'd just like to take that book and *burn* it. Yes, I would! So it couldn't contaminate minds. Now if you're interested, Susan, here's a book right here that I can *recommend*, a truly inspirational book, a lovely book, *The Man Nobody Knows*, by Bruce Barton. A lovely shining example. And this one too, *The Greatest Story Ever Told*, a lovely, reverent book."

"But I just think I'd like to read Miss Chase's," Susan said.

Aunt Maude sat down at her desk and latched onto her date stamp as though she had just taken a mouthful of milk of magnesia.

"I just want you to take these with you, too, Susan," she said, giving me an old bat of a stare. Probably thinking I was behind the whole conspiracy. "I'm sure dear Reverend Ogden would say the same if he was here to guide you." Susan got a big kick out of it and chuckled away all afternoon, until I got a little annoyed. I mean, Aunt Maude wasn't *that* comic.

But just the same I noticed Susan never said *Jesus Christ* or *God damn* like everybody else. Sunday School had really dinned that into her. It was only on a very rare day that she would use a swear word like that, and then she always looked sorry.

I never felt like getting very nosy about things like God and religion. I mean, I figured they had been going on so long there must be something to them, and anyhow, I had too many other things on my mind most of the time.

The only thing, all the time when I was a kid, the big scare of my young life was going to the dentist. Believe it or not, I prayed very regularly as a kid, and the big item in my prayer every night was: "Dear God, please keep me from having any holes in my teeth, no little teeny ones or anything, please God, very much. When the school nurse looks at us next month, don't have her find *any*, or any teeth to pull or anything. Please God, I pray more than anything in the world, dear, dear dearest God, please, please, please just this one thing, Amen."

Every night I spent about five minutes with God about my teeth, but every time the school nurse lined us up and began poking around with her old orange stick, whose teeth had more cavities than anyone's? Evelyn's. I suffered the tortures of the damned before I ever got to the old sourpuss's office, and if my mother had ever realized what it meant to me when she opened that downstairs door in Dr. Hooker's building and we climbed those grimy old stairs, and I began to smell dentist smell way down the hall, she would have turned me around and let my teeth decay on the stump.

Dr. Hooker hated it as much as I did, I guess, looking back on our little sessions. His smile was always pretty sick, the best he could do when he went into his routine, "And how's our brave little girl this morning? Going to sit right up and open wide like a good girl. Sure, sure we are. Now sit right back and I'll just put this napkin around your neck like this—it's just a *napkin*, kid, for God's sake, I haven't *touched* you yet!"

Anyhow, I kept on pleading with God for quite a long time, kids being pretty dumb, but finally I began to reckon that either my connection was poor or else He didn't give a darn whether Doc Hooker murdered me in his blasted old chair or not. So gradually I stopped nagging Him about it every night, and when I did that, gradually I stopped bothering to take up other things too, figuring if he wasn't going to pay attention, two could play at the same game.

Though occasionally when something really vital was at stake, like the State Basketball Crown, or when my mother thought she had cancer of the breast, I prayed away for all I was worth. It always made me feel better anyhow, and it certainly couldn't do any harm.

After that we drove almost all the way home, not exchanging a word. Headlights would come up the hills toward us and roar on by, and Francis's lights just went steadily along, like a brushful of paint unrolling, over the ditches, the woods where the pulpers had been and left piles of dead brush, the falling-down old gas station where the tame bear killed a man, and the orchards and the thick woods and the lawns and lighted houses and the grain-store windows and the furniture factory and the humpy little hills along the river where it was all farmland and rolling fields, with a hay baler lying beside the road, and along ten miles or so of electric fence, still light enough so you could see the white splotches on the cattle, along the blueberry barrens with NO TRESPASSING signs, across the river, the TOURIST'S HAVEN and the CRABMEAT SOLD HERE signs and the steamy white smoke from the outdoor cooking place, and on and on.

That road was such an old tiresome story I could start at one end and go the whole fifty miles in my mind, seeing every inch of it as though a movie camera was filming it.

In the distance near where we left the Turnpike I began to see the old neon lights of the beer joint flashing. Asher's Bar and Grill. Hamburgers, Lobster Rolls, Italian Sandwiches, Asher's Special Giant Wieners. Kreuger Ale in one window, with the little red juice running round and round, and Pabst Blue Ribbon nice and inviting above the door. I began to feel a little stir of interest in life again. Lights, food, a jukebox, and who could say what fascinating company might turn up! Anyhow, Asher was usually in the middle of some fuss or other.

One big trouble with us—we were hungry. I could smell those lovely fat hot dogs browning on the grill and see one oozing out of a toasted roll with mustard and piccalilli and dill pickles, beside a nice cold glass of Kreuger's. "You still alive, Susie?" I said.

There was bound to be someone hanging out there playing the jukebox, and practically anything was better than going home. I didn't hanker to face my mother until a new and brighter day had dawned.

"You want to stop for a hot dog before we go home? It's only about nine o'clock."

"Golly, you still got money?"

"God, yes," I said. "I can hardly stagger around with the money I still got."

"Well, okay, if you want to."

"Well, *you* want to?"

"Oh, I guess so. If we don't stay too long."

"It's up to you."

"Well, I'd just as soon. Only let's not stay too long."

"Anytime you want to leave, we'll leave," I said.

"Well, it's just . . . I mean, sometimes there's sort of a tough crowd in there . . ."

"Just Saturday nights. Look, if you don't want to go in, *say* so."

"Well, I do, Evelyn. You know I do. I *like* Mr. Asher, if that old Emile stays in the kitchen."

"Well, okay, then. And stop worrying. I'll protect you if there are any clowns around."

"Last time you went off with that bus driver—I didn't know where in the world you had gone."

"Oh for Pete's sake. Just outside to look at his bus. All the passengers were in there eating, weren't they? Maybe we were gone fifteen minutes."

She gave me a very accusing glance, which wasn't like her a bit, and in spite of myself I felt a little bit ashamed remembering that time.

"If Robert Taylor should be in there and ask me to dance, I'll say I'm Siamese twins and we've both got to," I said, teasing her. "I'll stick to you like glue, Susie, honest. Hope to die."

"Okay," she said. "Just so you remember that." She had certainly picked up speed in the talk-back department in one day.

Part III

Night

The jukebox in Asher's Bar and Grill was banging away with somebody like Wild Goose Frankie Laine. I thought he was keen singing that the first dozen times I heard it, but since then everything he sings sounds just the same, warmed-over wild goose.

Mr. Asher was puttering around behind the bar, and who was moping over a glass of beer way down at the end but Hine Hanscomb. "God bless our happy home," I said and poked Susan, but she had already spotted him and he her. Ships that collide in the night. They all but raised the flag and gave a forty-gun salute. "The day is saved, huh?" I inquired. But he was halfway across the joint to meet her and she was deaf, dumb and blind with happy confusion. Perhaps I should mention a big lesson which came to roost in my little brain that day and which I have traveled with ever since. It's pretty simple, but so are a lot of things that make sense. Everybody is a sucker for flattery. Of course you've got to figure out what his particular dish is, steak or mashed potatoes or tomato puree, but somewhere along the line it always works, if it's worth your trouble.

Hine got her by the arm as though he'd never seen a woman before, and started back to where he was sitting, with Susan trying to protest about my being there too and signaling that I should chase them.

"I'll be along." I let her see a little slight touch of sarcasm in my face for this fancy Siamese twin behavior, and pranced over to have a word with old Asher.

Two or three of the booths beyond the jukebox were filled and giving off commotion. When I took a better look, there was Jonas's big old Pepsodent leer raised up and grinning at me.

"Hiya, stormy weather," he yelled. "You look like you was going to cloud right up and spit snow. Don't you know it's summertime!"

"You'll never make me die laughing," I said.

"Come over here. We got business to talk over."

He had three dames with him in the booth, one I vaguely recognized. "How many strings you want to your bow, for God's sake? I'll see you in a couple of minutes."

I took a stool in front of Mr. Asher and leaned over and shook hands with him as though it had been months since we'd met. He was a funny little bird, shorter than me, and skinny. A strong wind could blow him away. He wore glasses with big horn rims, so that he had an owlish look, except that his nose was very pointed and quivered most of the time, and behind the glasses you discovered that his eyes were plenty sharp too, darting around and not missing a trick.

" 'Ere, h'Evelyn, what'll it be?" He came from London, England, and sometimes he talked so fast you couldn't understand a word.

"Two hot dogs and two glasses of ale. One for Susie down there."

"Yeh?" he said, cocking his head to look at them. "Ain't 'e the one to do the treating?"

"God, nobody's stopping him, Mr. Asher. Two dogs and two ale and I'm dying of thirst. We'll have everything on the dogs."

"Yeh?" he said again, giving me his sharp old eye. Then he bawled into the kitchen over his shoulder, "Emile! Fix two dogs." There was a waitress too, Sally, but she wasn't around just then.

Emile poked his head out and glared at us. He was practically a giant beside old Asher, weighing about three hundred, and as ugly as a caged polecat. Fat men are supposed to be jolly, but whoever thought that one up never met Emile.

"You want two dogs?" he said to me, as though I had asked him to dip into the garbage can with his bare hands. He and Asher were having a come-to, apparently, and weren't on speaking terms. At least Emile wasn't. His hair was very thick on top, bushy gray, and when he got excited, which was often, and began to shout at people, his fat old cheeks would shake and his bushy hair would shake and he would twitch his shoulders and go stamping around with his belly and his fat old behind quivering like jelly. His eyes were sort of lost in all the fat, but they saw everything, just like Asher's.

"Yes, and don't take all night, Emile, for Christ's sake." It was always easy to stir him up.

He took a gulp of air and looked at me as though he wasn't sure he ought to believe his eyes. Old King Slop, himself.

"You going somewhere?" he asked, real nasty. "Maybe you got some big engagement waiting. Okay, okay, I'll fix your wieners. I got nothing better to do in life than stick in this greasy hole cooking wieners. Hah! You think I got no more to me than that? I'd kill myself. Like *that*, I could go get me a pastry job in Boston. You know how much they'd pay me? Nah, you don't know. You see me in this run-down rat hole, you think I got nowhere better to go. Christ, there's nothing holding me back, you know that? Maybe I thought there was. Maybe I thought, *thought* there was some loyalty around here, maybe I thought I was appreciated for sticking around this joint, but I found otherwise."

He twitched his right shoulder up and peered at Asher, like a fat old queen. "*I found otherwise.*"

Asher turned around and all I could think of was a little yapping dog and a big surly Saint Bernard facing each other. "I told you it's all in your mind. In your mind. All made up," he sputtered. "Bless my soul, you'll 'ave me in my grave, between you. You're me mainstay, man, and you know it well enough. What the devil are you h'up to, between you, driving me to me wits' ends? Eh? Where's Sally, anyhoo? In the kitchen, there? She's wanted out here. They're h'after service. What's the girl think she's 'ired for, I'd like to know? Eh? There's customers waiting, man. Switch 'er out 'ere."

"What's the girl think she's hired for?" Emile repeated, pleased as punch. "That's just what I'd like to inquire! Me, that's what *I'm* wondering."

The shower was over, just like that. Emile lumbered back into the kitchen, humming under his breath, and old Asher winked and wiped the head off a glass of beer for me, and drew another one and took it down to Susan.

I didn't actually watch, but out of the corner of my eye I could see Hine jerk his head up and glare up at me, when Asher interrupted his monologue to say, "This 'ere is for you, miss, *she* says." Then he fished some coins out of his pocket and clanked them across the bar. "Get me another beer," he said, "and I'll pay for the three, hers up there too." He was really burned at my nicking him so easy, and it didn't take much imagination to see what a temperamental guy he was, with that black look and his eyebrows drawn together.

I sat and chuckled into my beer. It never tasted better. Susan was getting a big bang out of being the glamour girl, with me looking on, having her cigarettes lighted and her beer paid for and all that malarkey. I just hoped she didn't lose her hold on reality in regard to this joker, having her mind so much on sex problems and so forth. In a way I felt sort of responsible.

After a few minutes Sally appeared and grabbed an empty tray as though she couldn't call her soul her own. "Once in a while I got to go to the can," she said to Mr. Asher, keeping it low so I couldn't hear, but my ears are tuned to a low frequency. "That fat son of a bitch thinks he can boss me around, he's got a surprise coming. I told him, I said, 'I take my orders from Mr. Asher and nobody else.' I said. 'Keep your nose in a stewpot where it belongs.' God, he makes me boil."

"Easy now, easy," Asher soothed her. "Leave the battling to savages, gel, and we'll be better off, the lot of us."

He gave her arm a pinch and watched her all the way across the room, with his wary old eyes hiding behind his glasses, but I began to see light all the same. No fool like an old fool.

Sally was one of those carrot redheads, but she plastered on so much makeup, you probably never would have recognized her right after she washed her face. Anyhow, she knew her way around, mostly around the back, and between her and Asher and Emile, it was pretty easy to stir up something for entertainment around there, even if you paid for the beer.

Miriam Colwell

When I saw old Asher draw himself a glass of lager, keeping it down out of sight, I knew things were apt to start popping before the evening was out. They went at it about once a month, all three of them together.

I've heard a lot of people sit there at the bar and ask Asher how old he was and try to guess, but he never gave them a tumble.

"Old enough to know better," he always said, "like y'self." But other than on that subject he loved to tell you his life history. I must have heard it at least forty-eight times, but it was sort of interesting how the old guy had gotten around.

"When the old gel drug me to the preacher, I says jolly well for you, lady, and I 'ad 'er on a steamer to America before she knew wot was wot."

Since then, to hear him, he had just about kept the wheels of industry running, singlehanded. When they first landed he got a job as waiter in a hotel in New Jersey near where the ship docked. Then he moved to Brooklyn, New York, where his brother lived, and worked in a butcher shop.

Sometime along the line, he worked on the railroad, because he still had a pass that he once showed me. On the New Haven and Hartford railway. He loved to tell about the rooming houses where he stayed and the women that made eyes at him. There must have been a terrific mortality rate along that railroad, because every place he stayed was full of widows trying to get invited into his room or maneuver him into theirs. They talk about present-day morals, but it doesn't sound so different to me ninety years ago.

But he got an attack of rheumatism or something one winter, and had to leave off working outdoors, so he and his wife went down south and started running a laundry in a swank hotel. His wife was as happy as a clam down there, but he claimed he couldn't get along with the colored help. I'll bet he was a mean old cuss to work for. He could certainly iron shirts like nobody's business, starched and everything. I happened to go in there one day when Emile had to go to somebody's funeral, which they had all forgotten about till the last minute, and old Asher had an ironing board set up between the bar and the kitchen and he was slatting a big old steam iron around getting a shirt ready.

Sally was in the back trying to find Emile some socks and he was bawling at her from the bathroom, and poking his fat old lathered face out every five minutes to see if his shirt was done.

"Don't *scorch* it," he kept shrieking. "It's a lovely twenty-five-dollar shirt that I bought in Macy's *years* ago. Look the way you're letting it *hang!*"

"Never mind, never y'mind, man," Asher said, more to me than to him, not missing a tuck. "I've ironed shirts before ye was weaned, and I can spy a good one with the next man. Your dear h'old friend will be lowered h'into 'is grave and the dirt thrown h'on 'is face before you get into y'pants. 'Urry, 'urry!"

They were living down south when his wife left him to go back to England. He always got so riled at that point it was hard to tell what really happened, but one day he came home and found she'd taken the train out of there and most of their savings with her, and left him a note saying she was tired of his tempers and his drinking and of America in general. She was going back home and he could twiddle his thumbs for the rest of his life with his widows and his colored laundry help, for all she gave a tinker's damn.

Sometimes it would be ten thousand dollars or so she took and sometimes four or five, depending on his mood. By then he would get very melancholy and sorry for himself, telling about the plans they had made for opening up a nice little inn together to live out their old age where the climate was warm and so on, and how he had been reduced to owning a lousy beer parlor instead, and what a two-faced, scheming, small-natured, jealous, niggardly, foul-mouthed, self-centered, ugly-faced woman she had always been and would die being.

He still wrote to her once in a while and Emile told me she always sent him a Christmas present, every year. Mostly socks she knitted herself, which he wouldn't wear because they scratched his feet. Emile sent them out to Kansas City for his son to wear, being way too small for his fat feet. I nearly fell over when he told me he had a son thirteen years old.

"Oh my, yes," Emile told me very condescendingly. He was stirring up egg salad in a cracked old white bowl which he always used for everything because it had memories. He always used a big old tin shoehorn for a paddle. I suppose it had memories too. It always stuck in mine when I toyed with the idea of ordering a tuna fish sandwich or anything like that. But Emile was really very persnickety about his kitchen. A lot more so than my mother, for instance.

"Oh my yes, dear, I was once married. Oh yes. But I can tell you here and now, never again. Never. Not for yours truly. She came from Hot Springs, Arkansas. God knows what I ever thought I saw in her. But of course she *is* the mother of my only child. Loose! And *very* untidy in her personal habits, as I found out *right* away. It's a wonder I didn't kill that little tart. That's all she was. That's all she knew. Not one solitary speck of brain in her head.

"No, dear, I've never had one moment's regret about that one, and she knows where she can whistle before she'd ever get one red cent out of me. Was I born yesterday? No, dear, I was not!"

Old Asher was watching me watch him sneak swallows of beer, so pretty soon he set the glass right up on the bar and wiped his mouth.

"Been joy riding, heh? Where you been?"

"Up to the movies and 'round."

"You and 'er down there is good chums, hey, h'Evelyn? I've seen 'er in 'ere with you before. Well, a good chum is worth 'aving. Many a chum I 'ad meself in the old country."

"Sure," I said, holding up two crossed fingers. "We're like so, Mr. Asher."

"But ye're nothing atall alike, now that's a fact. From 'er looks I judge '*er* to be the shy kind. Some different from you, hey!"

Sally planked her tray down on the bar beside us and said, "Four more Budweisers for them comrades over there."

She began chewing on a fingernail while she waited, humming along with the jukebox.

A lot of people thought Sally was a tough customer, from her red hair and the way she always looked spoiling for a fight, which she was, but I always got a kick out of watching her tear around there. Sometimes she looked as wild as a bat.

"What you mean, they're communists, those four fellers?" I said.

"Christ's sake . . . how should *I* know?" She gave me that look of hers which some people took for meanness, but which really meant most of the time that she didn't know what end was up. Sally hardly *ever* smiled, except when she was drunk, and then it looked too lopsided to be cheerful. But it wasn't that she was unhappy or anything, just never got into the habit, I guess.

Thinking of a couple of people I knew, she had the right idea, and I wished she could spread the word around. For instance, baring your teeth like a horse about to whinny might look all right to another horse, but brother, it did nothing to me.

"What you mean, calling them comrades, then?" I said, just to needle her.

"Look," she said, tapping her fingernails along the bar, looking sharp as a porcupine. "Let me know in advance when I got to explain my every word, won't you?" Her fingernails were a purply-red color, just put on. Probably that's what she had been doing in the can.

"You better be careful, Sally," I said, "or they won't leave you any jingle, jangle, jingle."

She picked up the tray of sweating Budweisers and gave old Asher what passed for a pleasant look from her.

"Wise up, honey," she said. "You ain't so stupid as all that. From a mile away I can spot them kind. Big song and dance and then the four of them leaves me a quarter."

Sally's father was a bootlegger back in Prohibition. They lived way down on a point by themselves miles away from any other houses, and once when she was pretty drunk she began to tell me about the boats landing there, and the trucks coming down that lonesome narrow little road in the middle of the night to pick it up, and how something was always happening like a truck going off in the ditch and upsetting so she and her father and her mother had a whole load of booze to carry up off the shore and hide in the house. Before daylight. In case the revenuers came down for a look, and a lot of stuff like that. She was awful lonesome way down there with nothing to do and no other kids to play with, but her father used to give her boxes of fancy chocolates with rum inside, that he used to get at the big boats outside the three-mile limit, all crated in wood because they were so fragile. She even went out with him a few times, but not the time he got shot in the leg from a revenue cutter. It was foggy and he got away, but when he finally made it home, he had to run the boat right up on the beach and wait for them to get him out because he was so weak from losing blood and so forth.

Sally was only about nine years old then, but she swore to me that she got into the car and drove up for the doctor.

"Ma couldn't—hup—drive," she said, giving me a very tender, bloodshot smile. We were old buddies. There's nothing like eight or nine bottles of beer to make you buddies with most anyone. "Sure, I drove that car, Evlyngs—Evelyn. You 'lieve me, don't you? Christ, I could of drove a—hup—drove a God-damn motorcycle if I'd had one."

Another time when she got on a crying jag and men were no damn good for a half-hour or so, I sat in on her bed and listened to why it was she couldn't stand being alone a minute, and why she was such a sucker for guys with brown eyes or cowlicks, or for that matter, anyone in a pair of pants, and about the warp it put in your nature to be born with freckles, and how hard her mother used to work, making sour-milk biscuits every night which her father gobbled down a pan at a time, which was why she hated men. Jesus, don't ever get married.

I promised her I'd die first while she hiccoughed on my shoulder and spilled a glass of beer all over the foot of the bed, and first old Asher and then Emile and then half a dozen other characters were taking turns pounding and pleading at the door.

I learned a lot of very interesting things from Sally, about life and stuff, none of which she ever told me.

Emile came out of the kitchen with two wieners, and I must say he made the best ones anywhere, sizzling and covered with piccalilli.

Old Asher winked at me and took one plate down to Susan, but this time her big confusion didn't say a word. He just leaned on his elbow and looked along the bar at me as though everything was under control, his, and he couldn't be bothered. But I was too hungry to take that up at the moment, so I paid for them, giving him a long stare that said I couldn't care less, stinker.

Susan was wiggling around, trying to catch my eye to join them, but as an object lesson I pretended not to notice. If she worked up a little stew about my being sore, maybe next time she wouldn't forget her manners so fast. Not that I cared especially, but she was supposed to be brought up right and know things like you sat with who you came with, from habit. As I should know by this time, though, the sensitive artistic lame-brain type, like Susan, had to flail around and knock against everything in sight when they finally made a move, like a newborn gangling old calf, just to prove whatever it was they had to prove, which generally they hadn't decided at the time. Sometimes I wondered why in the world I bothered.

Then, sure enough, there she was at my elbow with a worried look, hitching down her shrunk-up old sweater, and trying not to let Emile and old Asher hear what she was saying to me, while they both had their ears pointed like collie dogs.

"Come on down with us, Ev. Golly, I didn't mean to . . ."

"In a minute I will," I said, just a shade on the chill side. "Just now I'm talking to Mr. Asher and company."

She gave them a weak smile, and hitched onto the next stool, looking so woebegone that I began to weaken. Her eyes looked as though she had used eye shadow. They always got like that when she stayed up past nine o'clock.

"Anytime you want to go home," she said, "I don't mind, Evelyn."

"Who wants to go home," I said, "for the love of Mike? We just got here. Your dog's getting cold down there. What's the matter with lover boy? He getting you down?"

"Oh no," she said. "It's not that, only I wish you'd, I mean . . . I . . . it's silly, you sitting up here by yourself."

She was worrying about *me* being by myself. It was pretty comical in a grotesque way. All of a sudden I felt jovial again. It may have been the food.

"Everything's jake, kid," I said, giving her a little pat on the shoulder. "It couldn't be a better world if it was real. Soon as I drink this I'll come on down and get acquainted. Now go back and eat your dog before old frog eyes does. He's got that lean and hungry look. Say!" It struck me very forcibly and I really had to turn around and take him in. "He *has*, Sue. I *knew* there was something. 'Yon Cassius hath a lean and hungry look. Methinks such men are dangerous.' You remember that, don't you? Old Shakespeare must have seen his great-grandfather around. Look at him yourself! I'm not saying it's bad, Sue, he's even cute in a sort of sad-sack way, but golly, I'm glad I remembered that. What was it in, *Hamlet* or something?"

Susan began to giggle, and then she couldn't stop, and it started me off too. For about five minutes we sat there quivering and sniggering until everybody in the place thought we were nuts. Especially old melancholy jaw himself.

He lit a cigarette as though life was too futile to bother about, and wigwagged at Asher for two more beers. Two, not three. I suppose he thought I wouldn't notice, but even in moments of merriment I kept in touch.

Emile had his arms folded, staring at us as though we were a species he had never encountered, like space women or something.

When old Asher came back he drew off two glasses of lager and slid one down the counter in front of Fatso, who grabbed it before the glass stopped moving, never taking his eyes off us, and half of it went down in one gulp.

To get myself under control I turned around to see what was going on. Eddie Fisher was singing "Tenderly" from the jukebox, which a deaf man a mile away could have heard with no trouble, and Jonas was dancing with one of his harem. At least it passed for dancing. Sally was sitting at the far end of the bar paying no attention to anyone but Eddie Fisher and her fingernails, and one of the comrades was getting up with his eye on Jonas's table. When the dame turned her head to look up at him, I recognized her right away.

She and her husband lived down home once for about a year. They were Navy and rented one of Tucker's crummy houses for seventy dollars a month, while he was stationed over at the Base.

No one around there has forgotten them, believe me. She had something to remember us by, too. From the front it wasn't noticeable, but when you saw her right profile, there were three long claw marks from her hair to her chin. Which she used heavy makeup to cover up. A new face was what she really needed.

When they first moved in no one paid much attention to the fact that they had a dog. There were a lot of dogs in town. Dogs and kids. So one more didn't cause any show of hands. Not at first.

Zida Coombs, next door to us, had a real cute little half-Airedale and half-spaniel puppy about six months old, and before long old Jetsam of the Navy was setting up shop on her doorstep. That mutt could furnish an education in basic sex without even putting his mind to it. Beside him the tomcats and the roosters might as well have been playing paper dolls. Fancy terms like *rutting seasons* meant nothing to that boy, he was on the prowl *all* the time, and twice on Sunday.

Zida's puppy was about the only honest-to-God female around, chiefly because Zida hadn't had time to take her to the veterinary, and anyway she wasn't old enough. All that summer Jetsam chased her around with blood in his eye, and Zida got so mad she had to go on a gall-bladder diet.

You couldn't blame her. He was as ugly as he was homely, a great big mud-colored ugly hound. It even got so he wouldn't let her use her own back doorstep. That was his station. To hang out clothes or get wood out of the shed or anything, she had to go out the front door and trudge way around the house.

People thought it was very funny when she started carrying a switch. They said, "Zida's always got to be stirred up over something," which was true, whether it was the neighbor's hens stepping over her boundary line—and don't think she didn't expect those hens to know where it was—or having to break up her son's big romance because the girl wasn't up to him, or carrying on a feud with a deer who ate the potato tops out of her garden but wouldn't turn up when she was waiting with a rifle.

Now it was Jetsam, and he had her so excited she stopped listening to *When a Girl Marries* and *Stella Dallas* because she just couldn't keep her mind on them. She thought every move that dog made was calculated to spite her, and she didn't want to miss any.

But it wasn't long before people stopped thinking it was such a big laugh. Jetsam wasn't the selfish type. When he got better acquainted he began to spread his personality around.

It was three-quarters of a mile between his house and Zida's, and he set up a personal patrol along the route. If he spotted someone doing their best not to look timid, he would bristle up in great style and go barking and growling and prancing right up to them, demanding what the hell they were doing in the street. Anyone who happened to have a newspaper or something of the kind in their hand he ignored for a poor sport, and jotted down a reminder to give them special attention tomorrow.

He had favorites too, like the old Taylor cousins, who were scared out of their shadows anyhow. If one of them decided after keeping watch all day without seeing him that it was safe to hurry down to the post office for the mail, which they hadn't gotten all week on his account, he waited until they were scuttling along under full sail and then he would appear, the hair standing up like a spine on his back, pawing and snarling along behind them until it was a wonder they didn't die of heart failure.

Of course there began to be a lot of talk around town that something ought to be done, but everybody waited for someone else to do it. The men thought maybe their wives would handle it, and the women thought it was a man's job.

In the barbershop they used to sit around making bets as to who he would bite first. Of course he had already nipped a few people, but not a real good vicious bite that might cause lockjaw or something.

When the Bos'n or whatever he was in the Navy stopped in for cigarettes, the talk would die out like a light. Until some horse's ass would say, "Where's your dog? He 'round today?" As though they were all dying to see him.

"The hound? Oh, he's out in the car. Guess he hangs out up this way quite a lot, huh?"

"Yeh, seems to."

"It's that bitch dog they got there at, what's their name—Coombs? The way I look at it, they ought to keep their bitch in the house. Know what I mean? A male's got to run. You can't pen up a male dog."

When my father came home with the happy news that Zida ought to keep Penny in the house out of the way and that would end all the trouble, I thought my mother would split a seam.

"Who says so, I'd like to know?"

"Why, this Navy fella. You can't keep a male dog from running. You got to shut up the female."

"Did you tell him how people was afraid to go out in their own dooryards around here?" My mother said, spitting fire. "Was he right there talking to you in the barbershop, for mercy's sake?

Did you tell about the poor old Taylor girls? Did you tell about the little Smith boy?"

"He seemed like a pleasant enough fella, himself," Pa said, kicking off his shoes, and pretending not to have his mind on the subject.

"The lot of you sat right there and never broached a word about what a terror he is . . . and the mortal fear we're in that he'll scratch some child's eyes out. You didn't, did you? Not a living word! You got to wait till it's too late and some young one'll lose their sight or their fingers or be maimed for life. Is that what you're waiting for? Is that the truth?" Ma was really getting warmed to the subject. "Or wouldn't any of you say Boo then, either?"

Then she remembered I was listening and slammed their bedroom door.

One night after that, though, when Jetsam tackled the old man himself on his way home from Tucker's with his arms full of groceries, and my father came tearing into the house like a wild man and grabbed his gun, ready to do murder there and then, she turned around and hid all his shells. She wouldn't even listen to him.

"The damn thing came sneaking up when I had my hands full . . . Look, there's his teeth marks, tore right through my pants! What'd you do with those rifle shells? I'll plug the son of a gun once and for all."

"That's just a playful nip, Father dear," I said. "Just to show you're friends. And anyway, a male dog has to run. You can't pen him up, you know."

I won't repeat his answer to that, but my mother gave us both a look that would have killed some people dead, and went off upstairs and never did tell him where she had hidden his ammunition.

Everybody in the neighborhood began to carry sticks and canes and newspapers, and the biggest subject of conversation was who he let alone that day and who he singled out. Big news item!

They must have had plenty of complaints, but it didn't do any good. The Bos'n was that kind, a nasty little squirt who sounded off all the time as though he had intelligence. It's so easy to fool the public. Whenever it was daylight he wore dark glasses to improve his appearance. It did, too. Anything did that covered some of it up.

But it was surprising the people who played along with him, just because he had a loud voice. They were all in the select group who didn't smell to Jetsam's taste.

"Why, that dog never bothers me. Brushes right by."

The Bos'n would stand there in front of the post office with one of these stinkers—and that's what I mean—and tell him how dear old lovable Jetsam wouldn't harm a fly even if it flew by shouting insults, and what a friendly old harmless he-man dog he really was.

And Stinker would say, "Sure, the whole trouble is people act scared of him. Now, *I* never pay him any attention and he never offers to bother *me*."

No, they said they couldn't tie Jetsam up, they couldn't think of confining an animal like that. Anyhow, he was different from other dogs, no pen could hold him. And I imagine his barking all the time got on their nerves so that when they let him out in the morning, they gave him a push up our way.

The Bos'n's wife was a little pleasanter to get along with or the lesser evil or something, but you couldn't get much more satisfaction. It was her husband's dog and they thought the world of each other, and her husband naturally just couldn't believe the nasty insinuation that Jetsam bothered anyone. She couldn't believe it either, because he was so gentle and affectionate around the house and always seemed very fond of children. My opinion was he was waiting for them to grow up so there'd be more of them to scare. And of course, she said, there *were* people who were silly about *all* dogs. There were people who had animal *phobias* and they were certainly to be pitied and she did from the bottom of her heart. Poor souls, going through life afraid of being bitten and such childish nonsense.

Her name was Luella, and when anyone took their life in their hands to stop at the house and complain, she would be very reasonable and soothing.

"Come to Luella," she would coo to old flea-bag, and she would rub his ears and let him drool on her lap to show how he loved affection. Probably polar bears love it too, and South American anteaters.

"If Mrs. Coombs would just keep that damn bitch inside, there wouldn't be any trouble!" she would say, and then offer them a beer.

At the time she was still keen about the Bos'n. *There* was a phobia. With some women the snakier a man is the better they like it. Until the fine day when they get the wrong end of the snake. He was the real strutting type, the kind who loves to stand up and be counted. Anywhere. Tail in, chest out, no guts, and you should catch me in my dungarees.

On Labor Day afternoon Jetsam bit Clancy Yaeger. Everybody said a taste of Clancy would finish any dog, but Jetsam's taste buds weren't very sensitive. Any number of people tried to run over him too, but he was craftier than they were. The town got to be a regular armed camp, with everyone taking sides, sympathizing or ridiculing or just not being on speaking terms.

Then out of the blue, with no warning at all, one day when Luella was riding along in the car with lovable old Jetsam, for some reason she didn't stop when he wanted, and he jumped right over into the front seat and let her have his affectionate nature right in the kisser.

It happened in front of Tucker's store, and Jonas was standing outside. He got her out of the car.

When the news got around there was as much excitement as V.J. Day. Someone even put up the community flag. Jonas took her home from the doctor's bandaged up like the Battle of the Bulge, which started before he could get his car turned around.

I guess the Bos'n still couldn't believe such behavior of Jetsam, and perhaps thought his wife fell in with a saber-toothed tiger. But as far as Luella was concerned, feeling was believing. And the slap Jetsam gave her must have contributed quite a lot for a while. Some people love to be convinced the hard way. Whatever happened in the little Navy love nest that night, it wasn't what you could call a calm discussion.

One of the neighbors finally called the state cop who said, Call the deputy sheriff, who said, Call the town constable, who said Damned if it was any of his lookout.

When the shooting started, someone else called the Base for the shore patrol or the fire department or anything, but they were all at the movies, so Luella and the Bos'n went ahead and made it a big night.

No one will ever know who shot Jetsam. Maybe he committed suicide, or died of ptomaine, but one of them shot him anyway for good measure, and not only that, there were bullet holes in practically every room in the house. One of them must have been a lousy shot, or they would both have woke up dead. The Bos'n did manage to get winged in the leg. The telephone operator heard him call the Base doctor and say to get the hell over there before he bled to death.

He only limped a little the next day when they moved out. She went first, bag and baggage, in the car, and he got a Navy truck to come move his clothes to the Base.

That was the end of that, except that Herb Tucker sued for the damage to the house, and Luella got a divorce.

Charlie met the Bos'n at a dance a while afterward and he said he felt a lot worse about losing Jetsam. He said, "Christ, chum, you can pick up a woman any day in the week, but where can you find a good ugly dog?"

In Asher's Bar and Grill Luella had on white sharkskin slacks that fitted before they got halfway 'round, and an off-the-shoulder black blouse with eyelets.

She was pretty well built, I had to admit, if you liked them on the overdone side. Down the bar, I saw Hine taking her in with that black glower of his and she wasn't minding it a bit, over the guy's shoulder. Dancing with one, she had to play across a crowded room with another one, and give Jonas a big come-on in between. It's a wonder the Navy ever kept afloat.

Beyond the comrades, there was a couple in the end booth, not saying much to each other. He wore glasses and sort of humped over his beer, and she was fidgeting around wishing something would happen. It probably would too, but ten to one she'd never know it. Though she wasn't bad in her fidgety way, I mean to look at. Probably living with her would be as restful as the inside of a busy pincushion.

Hine left his stingy old two beers and came up for Susan to dance. Which tickled her to death. He was a little shorter than she was, but they didn't look bad. He and I would have been just about of a height. And he danced better than I expected. I finished off my beer in a hurry, conjecturing what that might lead to, Susan having someone who could dance for a change instead of playing hopscotch all over the floor.

She was giving it a big deal, with her eye sliding my way to be sure I wasn't missing it, his cheek against hers and her head back, being very airy, as she had seen me a million times with Charlie.

She was right up there in the big spotlight. "Look, Ma, I'm dancing," and Queen of the May!

Asher slid me another Pilsner.

"On the 'ouse" he said. "Because I've always 'ad a sort of spot for you, h'Evelyn. You know the time-a-day, you do, gel. Well, your little friend h'is loosening h'up a mite, h'ain't she now!"

"Oh sure," I said, "Susie's human, same as the rest of us, Mr. Asher. It shows sooner on some than others, I guess, like measles or chickenpox."

He thought that was nothing short of riotous and had to take off his glasses to wipe his eyes. Also the lager was beginning to warm him up. He still kept one old eyeball rolling around after Sally.

"Oh God bless you," he wheezed. "Like the rash breaking out, she says."

Emile had gone wagging his fat tail back into the kitchen to get away from it all, but I could see the door heaving back and forth. He kept a stool back in the corner behind the jamb so he could sit and peek in through the crack. It was lucky people never wanted to eat much at Asher's. Emile just couldn't have fitted it into his schedule.

"But I'll tell ye, dear," old Asher said. "Between just the two of us, as are rare friends, now, h'ain't we? H'it's a fact that you're a kind I warmed to right from scratchy. Right from scratchy. But your little friend there, she's a different kettle of fish. She's got a stand-off look to 'er. Take a good while to get acquainted with '*er* kind."

That was putting it mildly, but I didn't feel like going into it. Anyway, our girl was getting fidgety. When you knew her as well as I did, it was very easy to tell. Though it wasn't always so easy to tell what about. I mean, it might be something between her and God that had just sneaked out into the open, as far afield as that.

But this time it was easy, it wasn't far afield or anything. She just wanted to call it a day and go home.

I guess it was natural. As fascinating as this wild man might be, pouring out the wonders of the world into her ear and giving her ego a big shot of oxygen, she'd had enough for one round.

It wasn't that I didn't appreciate her point of view, because as I said before, we were really pretty devoted to each other, odd as it may seem. I did appreciate how she felt. But here is a very strange quirk in human nature. On just such occasions as this when I knew she felt thus and so, and knew just why, I couldn't seem to do a thing about it. I mean, I *wouldn't*.

It was a pretty crude form of punishment, I guess, and not very hard to figure out if you can be objective about your own motives. I have never had much trouble along that line, though I am not bragging when I say so, simply stating something which is true, the same as the fact that I like spinach, and always have from a small child, though it's well known that children are supposed to hate it.

The simple reason—or maybe it's not so—why I had to punish Susie once in a while like this was because no matter how queer she was and so on and how nutty her conduct might be, I always had a sneaking suspicion, which I never dwelled on, God knows, that in some crackpot way she was one jump ahead of me.

So Susie wanted to go home, and kept giving me pleading glances which I ignored, as the fun was just beginning. People are very mean bitches to get along with, by and large.

The jukebox was blasting away. Eartha Kitt singing "C'est si Bon," but there was so much other noise now that everyone had gotten acquainted that Eartha was wasting her time.

Every once in a while a big trailer truck, maybe from Canada, maybe just from the lobster pound a couple of miles down, would go rumbling by, and the loose booth would rattle and wheeze. There was a window open and I could see a light blinking off on the water, where someone was fooling around in a boat. Which made me think it might be fun to go swimming, but Susie never would without a suit, naturally, with her inhibitions.

Anyway, there were a number of prospects right here that I hadn't taken time to explore yet.

"That's a pretty smart young feller there that's with 'er," Asher said, wagging his head. "I 'ad a word with 'im a while back. Yes, now a writer, eh? A smart lad—clever and all, 'ad 'is 'and in a good many pies . . ."

"Um-hmm," I said, without enthusiasm, "he's got derisions of grandeur is his trouble."

Emile put his head around the door like a turtle. "We'll all be in a book, dear. He'll probably make us all into re*pul*sive characters. Wouldn't you die!"

Then he popped back into his shell.

"My God, *you* ought to be in a book," I said to the door. "Except who'd believe it?"

To which the door made a very disagreeable and loud Bronx cheer, heard by all. Emile keeps a duck call out there tied on a string to his stool, and whenever he feels called upon, he can make an ungodly sound with it.

You might know who would respond to a noise like that. Jonas! Just like a homing pigeon, and laughing so he looked positively insane. An insane homing pigeon with teeth. Also he had Luella draped over one shoulder.

I wished to ignore him and his low sense of humor, so I said, "Why hello, Leola," as if we were long-lost sisters.

I sometimes loused up a person's name like that to get insight into their character. And anyhow, the way she was dolled up made me want to spit. "How's the world using you these days?"

"Why hello, dear," she said. "Long time no see. How's your mother, dear? Lordy, if I could just cook like your mother, Evangeline."

Evangeline! God, she really thought she was a keen cookie.

"For Christ's sake, relax, girls," Jonas said, being very witty. "I love you both. Let's admit it's bigger than we are."

Somebody dragged her off to dance just then, which was providential, and Jonas gave me a chance to check on his grinders, upper and lower. They were all there, just as flashy as ever.

"When am I going to get a thank-you, for God's sake, chasing my tail off with that bread? What would you do without Uncle Jonas, huh?"

"I'm going to pay you tomorrow," I said, keeping my distance, "just like I agreed."

"Oh, for Christ's sake, what's eating you, babe?" He gave me a very hurt look and I had to chuckle. As though he didn't have three women on his neck already. "That's better! Jesus, you and me don't talk about money."

I always thought Jonas was really wasted in this world. He should have been penned up and rented for eugenic purposes. To strengthen run-down strains and stuff like that. After one go, he would probably have had the women of run-down strains standing in line. The trouble was, I knew him too well, and anyhow, he was a little on the gamy side for my taste. It may surprise people, but I like men more of the refined type.

I took a small swallow of beer and decided it was time to come out of retirement and play a more positive role.

Jonas said, "Want to dance?"

"Not right now, honey. Later." I gave him a real warm smile, narrowing my eyes, to prove we understood each other, which God knows we did. "Something tells me I got fish to fry, honey!"

He swung around like he was stung and began giving everyone the once-over. "Love of God, who you got your eye on? Yeah, I see the son of a bitch. All I got to say, he ain't half the man I am."

He was pleased as a fool at how smart he was.

"What you want to bet I know which one?"

"I'm not interested."

"The guy back there in the gabardine suit," he said, grinning. "God, women is queer!"

Sally came lurching by and he jumped up and began to dance with her. They certainly made an unforgettable couple. Jonas's T-shirt was all looping out, and Sally balanced her tray on his head and began making a duet with Tony Martin, who was trying to sing "Change Partners." When she got potted, her eyes turned real shiny and glazed, and the mascara began to run.

Of course it *was* the one in the gabardine suit. I had filed him away for future reference when we first came in, but with so many things nagging me I couldn't get to it right away. Anyway, it's policy to pretend you couldn't care less for a while.

But I was tired of hibernating with other people's problems. So I sort of turned around and gave him a slow smolder. It was easy, like picking ripe raspberries.

In about one minute flat, he burst into flame and came right over, while I let old Asher light a cigarette for me.

Standing up, this guy was even better, thin and quite tall, with an Alan Ladd look, only not so pure. I mean, Laddie is probably okay if you know him, but I should care how many hens he raises, or kids, or how much manure he can pitch.

"What about dancing?" He had a smile that was real clear and crazy.

"If you like," I said casually, getting off the stool as though I didn't want to wrinkle my ball gown.

"Yes, I like," he said, sort of under his breath, and then we began to dance to "Change Partners"—which had been playing for at least one half-hour without interruption—as though we always had.

I began to feel very good. It was one of those moments when life was really worth hanging around for. Even the joint began to look bright, spindly old bar stools, specked signs, Sally with her hair over one eye, the booth that teetered, old Asher behind the bar with his glasses sliding down his nose, Susie watching me and pretending not to, Jonas and Luella, everyone, God love them—all of it looked just like a movie set, and I had the leading role.

That was the way it always was with me. One minute I wondered why I bothered to go on breathing, and then, bingo, it was my night to howl.

"What's your name?" he said. "Mine's Jim."

"Evelyn."

"You live around here, Evelyn?'

"Um-hmm."

He held me off so we could look at each other, and said, "No kidding. I was never so glad to see anybody in my life, Evelyn."

"Um-hmm."

So he stopped talking and began to dance, South American, very gaucho. It was really elegant, though God knows, I must have looked peculiar from the rear in those damn pedal-pushers.

He was my baby. I had to laugh at how nostalgic I'd been about poor old Charles tomcat earlier in the day. The hotel business was welcome to him, and his whole God-damn family. But I was too happy to wish him any hard luck. I was full of love and kisses. Nighttime was really my time.

Miriam Colwell

The rest of the twenty-four hours I could do without, especially morning. You could put me ten feet under, most mornings, and I'd hardly notice the difference. But about ten or so at night with a jukebox going and some people around and a few beers to relax everyone's nerves—then I stopped wondering what it was all about and took it as it came.

People get kicks different ways. Susan, for instance. Don't expect me to tell you how she gets hers—writing a poem, I suppose. Poor kid. Because what are kicks, anyhow? In my opinion, it's stirring up something between you and the general public, whoever he may happen to be. Which was why an evening like this at Asher's could turn into something with cream.

It was funny how I could get excited and stirred up and happy at night, but it never happened in the daytime. I tried to explain that to Susan when she once in a while was inclined to be bitter about my behavior, as for instance with the bus driver, but she would turn around and argue what great hilarious times people like the Ogdens and company had just sitting around chewing the fat.

Frankly, I can see it. And I'd rather shell clams. So they've got more money or brains or something, but it's the same old human nature, isn't it? Why not be honest and admit it? When I listened to Hine pretending he was all intellect, and so on, rattling on to Susie about the pictures he'd show her, I knew where it was leading even if she didn't. How dumb can you be?

It was leading right back to his room where there probably wasn't a thing on the walls but the wallpaper. I made a mental note to ask Susan a question sometime when she was feeling objective, which she hardly ever was, being so wound up in herself. All in the interest of education, as I was always interested in a person's reaction, no matter how cuckoo they happened to be. Like this: Would she get all hepped up walking her feet off in a museum the way I did meeting Jim and having a night on the town? If so, more power to her, only she better hurry up and find some museums. Time was a-wasting!

"Change Partners" finally stopped. Some kids who had just come in were hanging over the jukebox screaming over what to play next, but it didn't matter. Jim and I didn't need Tony Martin or anybody. He was a salesman for National Biscuit, and we already had a date for next week.

Luella was spreading herself all over the bar trying to get him to notice her. Just because a dog went berserk she thought she was Miss Rheingold.

The comrades were ready to go, and trying to signal Jim, as well as get rid of Sally. I guess they must have surprised her about the tip because she was all ready to go right along with them.

Jim was swearing because it was fifteen miles back to the Hitching Post where all the salesmen stayed, and he hadn't driven his own car over. I told him Susan and I came in her car, but he thought I ought to be able to borrow it to drive him home anyway. He was all for going over to ask her himself.

But affairs of the heart never affected my sense of logic. There might not be any gas stations open and there I'd be stuck with a free bus service. And also, my philosophy was, never let a man feel too sure of you, or anyone else either. Anyway, Francis was tired, and he didn't like people he didn't know. They always made cracks supposed to be humorous.

Jim kept whispering, "God, you're mean, Evelyn. What you carry in your veins anyhow, ice water? I thought you liked me. What is this, a big run-around, or what?" and more along that line, holding me closer and closer and starting to get very short-winded. Talk about dogs panting. I never saw a dog that could hold a candle to most of the men of my acquaintance. In that condition I'd certainly stop smoking.

I said, "Of course I like you, Jim, silly, but honest, Sue never lets me drive her car. Lamb, everybody's watching . . ."

It was very frustrating for him, because we couldn't even sneak outside for a private good-night. The comrades were all ready to breathe down his neck. Finally they started getting up, and he just stopped dancing and we stood there, looking soulful at each other. It would have made a wonderful scene. We stood there not hearing the jukebox yammering, or noticing the other couples bumping into us, or how everyone at the bar was watching.

It was a lovely, meaningful farewell. Luella was knocking herself out pretending not to care, tangling her fingers in Jonas's back hair, and Susan wore a very worried expression for fear I'd disappear with this guy and she'd have to let Hine drive her home. Which shows that she should have trusted me more.

"If you show in those God-damn pants next week, I'll drown you," Jim whispered very tenderly. I gave him my special slow glow, guaranteed to keep him eager for seven days or more, then the comrades dragged him away, and I wandered over to where Susan and Hine were sitting, looking as though the light had left my life forever.

Frankly though, this man-monster was getting under my skin. All evening I could have been a knot on the woodwork for all Hine appeared to care, and I couldn't help wondering whether he was slightly stupid or the crafty type. Now that he had seen me in action, I should be able to get some hint as to whether he was alive or dead. With most men it's not hard to tell.

Susan looked so relieved it was slightly embarrassing. "Who was *he*? Golly, he was a wonderful dancer."

"Ummm," I said. "Wasn't he cute!"

"My God, cute!" Hine said. "What's the matter, your vocabulary got malnutrition?"

The place this character and I could really get together was on a battleground.

Susan looked alarmed. "Oh, Hine. . . ." She probably had it all fixed in her head that we'd be the Three Musketeers or something.

"Look, pal," I said, "I happen to think he's cute. File your complaints as you leave. Why don't you just relax and enjoy life? What's your problem?"

At this he gave a nasty laugh, pretending he was Bogart. "Relax?" he said, as if he was God passing out free wisdom. "Why don't I relax? Don't you know, Evelyn, that struggle is the basis of creativity? Man was born struggling out of the womb, and dies struggling to keep on living, and in between he struggles even in his sleep. Fight the good fight, Evelyn. Praise the Lord and pass the ammunition. Beef and claw and slap the hand that feeds you, but for Christ's sake, don't relax!"

"That's *very* interesting," I said. "I'll make a note of it in the john where it'll do the most good."

He looked at me and really began to laugh. His face was quite human when he stopped being a junior Humphrey.

"Great!" he said. "Do that and sign my name. Don't be a plagiarist."

Whatever that crack meant I never found out, as Jonas came up and tried to climb into my lap.

"For God's sake, you're a big boy now. Go sit on Luella," I told him.

He made a face and pointed out toward the back. "If I'd known you was coming, I'd have flipped the switch on the bitch," he said, grinning, as though he was John Greenleaf Whittier.

"Don't waste that lousy line on me," I said to him. "Remember when you and I were young, Muggie."

"Hey, how about you and me dancing?" he said to Susan, as though she was just another girl. I got ready to catch her when she fainted, because in her right mind she was scared to death of Jonas. She told me once it was mainly because when he grinned at her, it was as though he knew more about her than she did herself. That was said in a weak moment and afterward she hardly spoke to me for a week, she was so undone. At confiding such an intimate revelation! Brother. And all the time I thought it was because she was shocked at my breaking into the library nights for necking parties.

Charlie and I and two other couples did that for a while because it was naughty, but it smelled of glue and was cold as ice, and anyhow, reading tables are certainly not meant for such purposes.

Come to find out though, Susan had never even heard of it until I told her.

"Okay," she said to Jonas, and smiled at Hine, and there she was, dancing off like anyone else, and furthermore, enjoying it. It surprised me so I just sat there and meditated. After a minute or two I noticed that Hine and I seemed to be glaring at each other, and I pulled myself together, as above all I didn't want him to get the impression I was mad for his company.

"You two are a funny pair," he said, and actually offered me a cigarette.

"It's all in the eye of the beholder," I replied, offhandedly. I heard someone say something like that once and ever since, it kept running through my head.

Very few people when they look right at you won't smile or at least look friendly, I mean when it's just a casual conversation, but he lit my cigarette and we gave each other the old business over the match and, frankly, I couldn't tell whether he wanted to be palsy or clout me with a tire iron. It was unnerving, especially after the day I'd had.

"Maybe I had you down wrong, Evelyn." He talked so low I only heard about half he said. "After a remark like that, I have to admit maybe I was wrong about you."

"Oh, don't bother," I said. "Don't wear down your system admitting mistakes. If you'll excuse me, I got to go talk to Emile."

Always leave a game when you're winning. Emile was sneaking himself another glass of beer, and sending dirty looks down toward the end of the bar. Old Asher and Sally were in a huddle down there, having a confidential talk, which included Asher's feeling her here and there to make sure she was listening. Sally's eyes were about as focused as a seed potato, but she was giving it the good old try, being quite girlish in a drunken way.

I sat down on the stool in front of Emile and felt at peace with the world, though slightly hungry. Jim was in my future, and Charlie was a dear dead figment of the past. Progress had certainly been made since morning, even if my main problem of money and what next and so on was still hanging fire. After all, if a girl used a little ingenuity, who could say? One reason I liked beer was because it always made me more optimistic.

I could feel Hine staring with that scowling superior look of his, and that added to my general feeling of well-being. Maybe be didn't enjoy being walked out on, I hoped.

For a few minutes I just sat there savoring my frame of mind, and listening. It was pretty noisy with the jukebox and all the yakkety, yakkety, and every once in a while Asher's radio behind the bar would find an opening and be heard blatting something about a new Ford or an international conference or just dance music.

A million moths were fluttering around the light by the screen door, and just outside I heard someone laugh and then the smash of a bottle.

I felt really good, with that feeling I sometimes have of being the only one in a place with eyes and ears, as though I sort of hold all the strings.

I gave Susie an encouraging glance over Pepsodent's shoulder, and she took heart and began chattering to him as though they had a million things in common. Poor old Susie, she was tired. I suppose writing two poems in one day was pretty wearing. But sometime she would no doubt hark back and thank me for an invaluable part of her education. Rubbing shoulders with the underworld—Jonas, for instance. An experience like that could easily be unforgettable.

Emile was humming away to himself, looking so relaxed that I thought I had better recall him to reality.

"What's going on around here?" I said. "Don't tell me Pa Asher's fallen for that dope of a Sally!"

That recalled him all right and he twitched around so he couldn't see the horrid sight. "My God, Evelyn, I've just about taken a bellyful. They just offend my sense of decency. Look at her!" he rolled his eyes like a dying duck, and looked quite a lot like her. "You know what she's after, don't you? She thinks the old bird'll leave her his property. The tart. The drunken bitch. My God, don't she turn your stomach? And the old fool's getting all lathered up, my senses, isn't he going to give her a big time! Oh, my conscience! She'll have to be drunker than she is now, I can tell her that.

"Just between us two, Evelyn, I am *some* surprised at that man. Asher and I have been very close, you know. Very close. It just don't do to put your faith in anyone."

He was working up to a good cry. "There's very little gratitude around here," he said. "Hand me one of those napkins, dear, no, just *one*."

While he was blowing his nose he didn't miss a dropped stitch anywhere in the place. Emile was sort of a study himself if you were interested. I guess he had been all over the United States at one time or another, but he came up here from Florida one year with the Baxters, who own a big summer place on Gull Island.

They had hired him in Florida as their cook, and everything was very lovely for a while. He had two Filipinos to help in the kitchen, and the Baxters appreciated him all over the place, and there was always a lot of liquor around, easy to get at.

The cook before Emile had been a very smooth Italian lad, with brown melting eyes. I had seen him a couple of times in the summer. But he developed woman trouble, too many at one time was his trouble, and as the mean old gossips had it, that included Mrs. Baxter. All this led to his getting into a fight one night in Miami and landing in a hospital with a few slices missing and a broken hand, which cooked his cooking.

That was when they hired Emile, and after the first week Mrs. Baxter told him what a relief it was not to have a woman always hanging around the back doorstep.

I happen to have the low-down on the whole affair because Poop Casey is their caretaker over on the island. Poop and Dad were in the Revolutionary War together.

It seems Mrs. Baxter didn't want to leave Miami with poor Sully in a hospital. It wouldn't be cricket, as he had been their cook and so on, to go north and leave him in a helpless condition. So why didn't Mr. Baxter and the rest of the household go along and she would do her duty by the poor boy and fly up later. But Mr. Baxter didn't care for that kind of cricket. I guess he wasn't much of an old boy for games of any variety. With the result that poor Sully was left with just nurses to play with and he probably did all right, from all I've heard about nurses.

Mrs. Baxter's spirits were very low when they got to the island, Poop said. She didn't even give him hell for losing half the rose garden, which there was no need of, as he said himself, not to them naturally, if he had just covered it up.

She didn't go near the kitchen either, just sent Emile orders by one of the Filipinos. Most of the time, according to Poop, she lay around on the lawn in a bathing suit, lapping up martinis. Old Money-bags was about sixty years older than she was when they got married.

But as far as living on an island went, it didn't mean a thing, because they had a bridge built right over to the mainland. Fatso was really in clover, with a couple of slaves to boss, no one poking around to make sure he was washing his hands, and a Filipino to pour him in bed when he got sozzled.

Then over Labor Day the Baxters gave a party. A real wingding. Poop had to make a big beach fire the day before and bake bean-hole beans and steam clams and roast corn and God knows what-all, and late in the afternoon, all the guests came streaming down on the shore, really roughing it, with about a dozen extra waiters to tend bar, and a trio strumming on guitars and singing, and Poop's son running the speedboat for anyone who wanted to live dangerously.

I forget how many empty cases of whiskey and gin and what-all Poop had to drag off afterward. He and Dad sat and hashed it over like a couple of old harpies, but statistics mean nothing to me. The main thing was that everyone got boiled, including Mr. and Mrs., the trio, even Poop. Though with him it's hard to tell the difference. By midnight most of them had either passed out or gone home. Things had even quieted down in the kitchen, except for Emile and a couple of larks from the trio. When what should happen but Mrs. Baxter comes marching in, somewhat the worse for wear.

Miriam Colwell

"And who have we here?" she inquires very regally, and grabs Emile's arm just in time to keep from falling flat on her face.

Emile says she just had on a dressing gown that wasn't fastened. But Julio, the electric-guitar player, claimed she had on a bathing suit. Poop, who had been having a nap outside, under the lilac bushes, said she didn't have on anything, but you can discount that. The little banjo player that Emile had his eye on, Willie, said she was dressed just like all evening, in an off-the-shoulder, very cool creation, striped blue and black.

"Oh yes," she says, "the lovely boys who sang for us. Those jackets are so attractive—so wonderfully becoming. Tell me your names, do. Can't we just relax and all be friends? It's so tiresome in there. A deadly bore, really. I think everyone's passed out, but I'm so glad I found you boys still here. We must all have a drink."

Emile was still sort of holding her up, speaking of leaning on broken reeds, but she had gotten her eye on Willie. It was certainly his day.

"Tell me your name, dahling," she said to him. "I thought your voice was heavenly. Sing something for me now, won't you? Just you alone, because it's so late. Do you know 'Macushla'?"

Willie was as drunk as anyone else, even if he did look about sixteen and had foot-long eyelashes, so he began to sing "Macushla" to her. Right there, surrounded by dirty dishes and empty bottles.

"Pour us all a drink," she said to Emile, and changed over to hugging the Frigidaire. It was just about Emile's size anyway.

Then Julio, the electric-guitar player, chimed in too, and then Mrs. Baxter herself, and pretty soon the three of them were entwined like valentines, really sending. Probably Emile has no ear for music, because he began to get very peeved.

From all the accounts I have pieced together, they had two or three more rounds, while going through every song that had ever been written, with Emile standing off in a corner by himself really working up a temper. Finally he began to tell them right out loud that he was the boss in his own kitchen and he was God-damn sick and tired of being pushed around, and why didn't certain people stay in their own part of the house, and stop hobnobbing with the hired help and furthermore acting like a tramp.

Maybe that last she had heard before, because Poop said she straightened up like an icicle and went into a very queenly act. It must have been pretty humorous if you could have been a fly on the ham or something and taken the whole thing in. There she was swaying around amongst a mountain or so of dinner plates and cups and stuff, reading Emile a very sharp sermon on the fact that she would not stand disrespect from servants and he'd better mind his tongue in her presence.

Then having shut him up in a style to which he was unaccustomed, she and Willie decided to step out to see the moon, with little Willie grinning like a fool. This on top of everything else really broke the old camel's back.

Poop, naturally, was glued to the back window, taking it blow by blow, and he says Emile began to shout, "Why don't you go back in there where you belong?" and that he grabbed a bottle and started waving it around in a very menacing manner.

That dame must have loved a good fight as much as other things which she had on her mind, because she put Willie aside, eyelashes and all, and opened up the shore batteries on old Fatso.

What Poop could understand of her remarks he said were very expressive, but she also went into French and Italian and probably Latin before she ran out of breath, paying no heed to the way Emile was winding up with a Vat 69 bottle or the look in his eye, which must have been real rare by that time.

When she ran out of French swear words she started off on a new tack to keep the boys amused, though I doubt if they were exactly yawning on the edge of boredom. She went up close to Emile and gave him a real poisonous sweet smile.

"I don't understand you, Emile," she said as though it kept her awake nights. "I try to understand all my servants, but you represent an insurmountable obstacle. Are you immune to women, Emile? Have you been inoculated against the opposite sex? Is there some new medical discovery I haven't heard of? Have you heard of it, Willie, dahling? Isn't he a lamb, Emile? Look at those heavenly green eyes. Just like a beautiful cat I once had that I simply adored. But Emile, I'm terribly concerned about you. Really, I can't have someone in my kitchen who seems so strange and inhuman. It's too killing . . ."

Poop swears she began to stroke old Fatso's arm, but Poop gets carried away sometimes.

"Emile, tell me something—have you ever possessed a woman, a person of the opposite sex? Feel free to unburden your secrets to me, Emile, utterly horrible though they probably are. I know a perfectly dear psychoanalyst I can send you to."

Then she got tired of that and backed off with a really mean snobby stare, as though she couldn't believe the cat would drag in such an object. "Put down that bottle this instant and stop acting like a drunken fool. Leave this room immediately. Get out of my sight! I can't stand your fat foolish face."

Old Emile put down the bottle. As hard as he could right into the sink, which was full of dishes and silver and glasses and so on, and then he nipped over to the meat block and picked up a big meat cleaver. "You rich bitch," he shouted. "You dirty-minded little whore. You got no breeding, you got no background; all you got is a busy tail."

With that she winged a full stack of dinner plates at his head and took off three jumps ahead of the cleaver. It must have been real bedlam around there for a couple of minutes, and off they went, tearing up the driveway, while those big brave men stood there shedding broken china.

"Why, you know this bad leg of mine," Poop said. "Anyways, a deer couldn't have caught up with them."

In a minute the planks on the bridge began to rattle and away they went up the hill on the other side, with Emile screaming like a banshee.

To this day I never see her driving around in that Lincoln convertible, with the back full of pedigree hounds, giving the poor pedestrian her big lord-of-the-manor smile, without thinking of her steaming along that old twisted road that night in the dark.

To end this gruesome tale, he never caught up and they lived unhappily ever after. Being so fat he couldn't catch anything much but a cold, which she would have been glad to know at the time. Anyway, he used up too much breath screaming. But she ran the whole way out to Parkers', which is the first house, three and a half miles, thinking the whole time he was right behind, and banged on the door until they came down and let her in.

Well, those are the problems people with money run into. Having to hire cooks and give parties and so on. Blessed be the poverty-stricken.

They didn't have Emile arrested as you might think, just severed the connection.

Sometimes I couldn't help wondering what would have happened if she'd stubbed her toe.

"Look, Emile," I said, "things are tough all over. You got to have a philosophy of life. What's your philosophy of life, Emile? Don't tell me you haven't got one at your age!"

"He'll find out," he said, blinking his little narrow eyes. "Let anybody kick me once, and they'll find out real quick, girlie. C. Emile Jones don't take shabby treatment lying down in the dirt asking for more, no indeedy. As more than one has found to his sorrow, I may say."

The jukebox stopped and the screen door slammed. The radio on the shelf behind the bar filled in with a baritone singing "Ave Maria," but no one noticed.

Old Asher came frisking up, with his glasses dangling and all seven wisps of hair standing on tiptoe.

"Now then, we're 'aving a nice party," he said, happy as a lark. "Ooh, it's a grand sight seeing young people enjoying themselves." The record might be a little cracked, but the old boy was balling along just the same. "H'and your little friend has come h'out of 'er shell; h'it's a marvel!"

Emile had his arms folded and his lips padlocked, Chief Plug Ugly himself, but old Asher had him over a barrel as well as Sally, and don't think it hadn't occurred to him.

"Look at the face on 'im!" he said. "H'out with it. What's yer complaint? H'it's no time to look lugubrious. I'll tell ye, now. It's a good meal is what we need. Why, I'm close to famished. What do you say? Don't stand there like ye was stricken! Get out that steak I brought from town yesterday. And h'Evelyn 'ere and 'er little friend shall eat it with us, all good friends together, like in h'old England."

"Oh, golly," I said with my mouth watering, "I don't know; it's pretty late, Mr. Asher."

"Sure, sure," he said. "Wait till you see it, she's a beauty, gel, fit for royalty. And you're an 'undred percent, h'Evelyn, see, that's what I say to meself, h'about you. And your friend there, too. Yes, yes. Though in reality, as to 'er, there's no telling. She's not for easy reading, eh. Sure, I see 'em come and I see 'em go."

At the mention of food, especially steak, Emile unbent and began to look positively ecstatic. It sounded good to me too. All I'd had for hours was a lousy hot dog and a few bushels of pretzels.

"What would be your desire, princess?" Emile inquired. "String beans or buttered carrots? Also a choice of french fries or fried potatoes. What will your highness prefer?"

"Get it ready, get it ready, carrots, beans, whatever you got, man," Asher said, shooing him away like a flock of geese.

So Emile beat it into the kitchen and began to throw all the pans onto the floor and jump on them by the sound, but I guess it was just the way he operated getting a meal, as Asher didn't seem to notice.

Some joker with a flaw in his humorous side started "Change Partners" again. Even Tony sounded pretty tired of it by now. Susan got up and disappeared in the direction of the Ladies.

"Look," I said to Mr. Asher, who was all ready to dive into his autobiography, sparing no details. "I better go tell Susie, and see if she'll stay."

"Sure, sure, okay," he said. His face was pretty red and he pushed at his glasses so that he could approximately see through them. "Tell 'er h'it's just good friends together, see? That gel's got upbringing, tell 'er now. A good steak and good friends, eh! Where's the fun in eating by your lonesome? There's plenty of that to be 'ad. Go tell 'er the old duffer's got 'is 'eart set h'on . . . h'on the honor of 'er company!"

Susan was in there so long I began to think she was taking a nap. The john was down at the end of the building between Emile's bedroom and Asher's. Sally's was across the hall. I didn't knock or in any way hurry her up. Activities connected with plumbing upset her so, and she was always so sort of furtive about them that I just waited, not wanting to badger her.

Anyhow, it was restful to just lean against the radiator in the hall and think things over. It was one of my social trademarks, to disappear every once in a while. It kept people guessing. In fact, I was so quiet that she was amazed when she finally opened the door.

"Oh golly, Evelyn," she said. "Why didn't you knock or something?"

"Why for? I'm in no rush. Look, honey, you're having fun, huh?"

"Well, sure," she said. "I guess so, but it's getting awfully late. I think we ought to be going home. Honest I do. Let's go home, Evelyn."

"Well, I'm all ready to go home," I said, "only old man Asher has invited us to a steak supper, on him. 'Course, we don't have to, but I'd hate to hurt the old gink's feelings. Have him think we're too good or something."

"Oh Lord!" she said. "Well . . ."

"We can leave just as soon as we eat. And how could we go to sleep on empty stomachs? It's not good for anybody to go to bed hungry. That's how to start ulcers and cancer and stuff."

She began to giggle, though still with a sort of worried look. "You know what you do?" she said. "You rationalize all the time."

"Oh ducky, so now I know," I said. "Is that from his lordship, the horse's ass?"

She giggled again. I guess she'd gotten her second wind. Or maybe Hotshot had slipped a slug of adrenaline into her beer.

"No," she said. "I thought it up myself." She pawed the floor a minute and then made a big revelation. "He . . . he wants to take me home."

"No kidding?" I said. "I can't believe it."

"But we'll go pretty soon, won't we?"

"Absolutely," I said. "You may rely upon my word of honor."

I was pretty relieved and actually pleased to know she wasn't playing around with man-monster at least that evening, because in a way, you might say I was responsible. Being, as far as life was concerned, much the older of us two.

It sounded like a madhouse out in the joint. Someone had turned the radio on loud so it was competing with the jukebox as well as with the rest of the barnyard. On one, some yoo-hoo girls like the Andrew Sisters were murdering "A Pretty Girl Is Like a Melody," though it's a miracle you could tell, and on the other a band was being very philharmonic. Besides this, everyone was yammering or laughing or banging down a glass. Oh glorious summer, *nuit beau, de fête joyeuse*.

"Just remember," I said, feeling sort of carried away and fond and so on, "Mama's got her eye on you. Just tell that gazebo not to try anything funny."

She leaned over and gave me a quick little peck on the cheek. I nearly fainted and so did she, except that she didn't wait, but beat it back to The Rainbow Room. With her, such demonstrations of affection were as likely as snow in July, and hen's teeth. It really got me where I lived. I mean, if the need arises, and somebody needs to be taught a lesson or something, I can whip up a passion for most anybody, including a dead horse, but that's strictly off the cuff. This nice warm feeling between Susie and me was for real. All the time in the john I was brimming over with sentiment. If the truth be known, I'm a very sentimental person.

When I went back out, there was Jonas with his teeth aglow, so we began to dance. It was easier than arguing. When some couples get to a certain stage it makes me hysterical to watch them. That was the way with the couple in the end booth, the one with the woman who was over-activated in one or other of her compartments.

Now they were both polluted with Kreuger's and holding each other up all around the floor, under the weird impression they were following the music. Both of them had that look of a dead flounder primed with aphrodisiac. If you wonder how I know, think of a dead flounder, then think of a flounder more dead than alive trying to look sexy. That is an expression a great many people of my acquaintance assume at one time or another and it sends me. I really lose control. I mean, I have to go off in a corner and give way to convulsions.

Perhaps you've been wondering about all the beer I've mentioned up to this point. To put it briefly, I never drink more than two and a half beers at a time. A lesson I learned early in life was namely: It's more fun to keep track of what's going on, and also, it's very easy to make a complete clown of yourself. It's unfortunate that most people never learn this early or late, but I guess if they did, it wouldn't be so entertaining for the rest of us. What I did when people like old Asher, bless his heart, kept pouring me more beer, I watered his geraniums, and also kept another glass nearby which I contributed to from time to time.

You'll notice if you ever try this that someone always comes along and picks up the extra. "This is where I left my glass," they'll say, or, "Hey, what you doing with my beer?" I go through sometimes six extra glasses in one evening.

Jonas was muttering away in my ear, "When we going to get together kid, huh? You and me, huh? Look, when you going to stop fooling around with boys and find out what a man's like? Get wise to yourself, baby. For Christ's sake, what's Charlie Monroe got to offer? I bet he ain't even fully developed."

Miriam Colwell

"You got the most one-track mind I ever met."

"Fighting trim, kid," he said grinning. "No kidding, you and me would make a lovely couple."

I let him muddle on like that for a while because Luella was really breathing fire in our direction, but as a matter of fact, I could feel an attack of virtue coming on. I have such moments occasionally, and brother, while they last, which is never long, I really live them up. Bean bags at the Christian Endeavor is strictly my speed.

"Jonas," I said close to his ear, "sometimes I wonder if you have proper respect for the opposite sex."

"Depends on how much sex they got," he yapped right back, beaming from molar to molar. One thing you could say for this Active Andrew, he never looked downhearted or discontented. Never in my remembrance. Occasionally disappointed, but never glum.

Jonas was also pretty interesting from the human-nature standpoint. The fact is, he had been engaged for over a year to a very nice-type girl, Flora Sibley, who was a district nurse. Flora was a good-looking dame, and she flew around visiting the sick and so on like mad in a maroon '49 Mercury convertible, but never with the top down. Too busy, I guess. She was the type who read stories in *Good Housekeeping* and *The Ladies' Home Journal* about girls who never let boys get too fresh until after the ceremony. Also she lived at home with her parents and was the soul of propriety and the flower of young womanhood. Don't ask me how she happened to fall for Jonas. I'm only telling you it happened. Attraction of opposites. But the real screwball part is this: Flora was the one person in the county who didn't know what a fiend on wheels he was. *She* thought he was purely wonderful. As far as she was concerned, he didn't swear, drink, or pick on dumb animals. Some people certainly love to kid themselves. As far as to make it their life work.

Of course, plenty of people tried to wise her up, by dropping word that they saw him coming out of the movies with another woman—it turned out to be his sister when she asked him—or that his car was up at Asher's Bar real late the night before—he was there trying to get his uncle to go home, or else it wasn't his car at all—and these catty people turn out in her opinion to have very malicious, troublemaking tongues, as well as bad eyesight.

Jonas took her out a couple of times a week when there wasn't an epidemic or something, and had supper at her house every Sunday night. He thought the world of her, as he told me himself in a weak moment, but anyone knows a tomcat won't change his habits just because there's a nice warm bed behind the stove. Not till winter sets in, anyhow.

"What do you know!" he said, all of a sudden. "There goes Susie and the Professor. Going out to count stars, I bet yuh!"

"Where? Where are they?"

"Sneaked right out the door, kid." Just then the music stopped. "Susie ain't so bad when she limbers up a little. I always thought she was stuck on herself."

I was really upset. "Look, Jonas, I'll be right back."

"For Christ's sake," he said, "what are you, a nursemaid or something? Okay. Papa'll come too!"

That was just splendid any way you looked at it, so I towed him over to the bar before he knew what was up, and there was Luella.

"Thanks for the loan-out," I said. "He's all yours."

"Oh, I'm well aware of that," she said, as unpleasantly as possible, "but I adore the way he lets children monopolize him."

"Where you h'off to?" old Asher bawled.

"Be right back." At the moment I couldn't even wait to slap the bitch down.

"You'll make some chaperone!"

"What you so worried about—he ain't even her size!"

But I left them to it and scooted for the door. Outside on the step I took a moment to figure what I was so haired up about. I couldn't believe she would run out on me, but she had been in a very queer mood all day, and with this thought in her mind, that she had to find out about life and so on, there was no telling. And this guy was so sneaky, I dreaded to think what might happen.

After all, I was fond of Susan and wanted no harm to come to her, and Hine Hanscomb might as well have had harm written all over him. He was harm personified.

I may as well add too, as long as this is an honest account, that curiosity was breaking out all over. I wanted to know how these two oddballs were going to wind up their evening.

They were way over on the far side of the parking lot standing by his car, so I ducked quietly from car to car, keeping out of sight, until I got to Francis, who was only two down from his. By the time I got there I was hysterical with amusement at this cowboy-and-Indian game, and felt practically carried back to childhood.

Right away I could tell that she wasn't pulling a fast one, but had just walked out with him to say good-night. He was really on his way, as he had borrowed his cousin's car and told her he would be back by ten. Which proved what I already thought about his trustworthiness, being half-past already.

It was a very pretty night, with a lot of stars overhead. The air smelled good. After a few hours in that opium den, you needed a breath of air.

He was still trying to persuade her to go home with him, and she was still using me for an excuse.

I heard him say, "What is this, anyhow, a Trilby and Svengali setup?"

How he loved to fling around unintelligible names to keep people from knowing what he was talking about. Just as it happened though, my mother had that book, which I came across once as a small child.

"Look," he said, "for the love of God, be reasonable. Evelyn would leave you flat on a minute's notice. You admitted it."

That surprised me. To know she was capable of such a snide remark. Though possibly it might have happened.

"I don't want to leave you here in this gin mill. My God, Susan, they're a cheap bunch in there. You don't belong in a place like this. Maybe your girlfriend eats this kind of stuff up, but not you, Susan. You're going to need more out of life. Look, I know you have this stupid feeling of loyalty, but use a little common sense. What about your aunt? I bet she's lying awake right now, worrying about you."

He was on a very smart tack there, but not being as clever by about ninety percent as he thought he was; instead of pressing it, he started kissing her.

I was amazed that she just sort of let him. It really was just as well that I was there, as an invisible chaperone. But being no eavesdropper by nature, God knows, and as my feet were killing me, I sat quietly down on Francis's running board and left them to it. Francis was very pleased to have me there and we sat communing and watching people flit past the windows inside the joint. A man from Mars would certainly have gotten a headache trying to figure what was going on in there.

Charlie was completely flown from my thoughts; at least, I mean, I could think of him with no interest whatsoever, beyond friendship. But sitting there in the dark with Francis groaning with age, and knowing about ten feet away Susan was finally acting almost like other people, I suddenly felt pretty sad. It seemed like the end of an era and all that. Nothing was going to be the same anymore. I knew it, whether anyone else did, or not.

A car pulled in and parked and turned off its lights. In a minute the screen door banged.

They were still in a clinch back there, and I must admit Hine knew what he was about. Life with Edgar was never like that, believe me.

"Susan, come on home with me," he said very forcefully in a tender way.

I was compelled to crawl around to Francis's near side as their voices dropped, due to all this passion.

"You're not nervous at going with me, Susan, that's not it, is it? Darling, look at me; you're not as silly as that, are you, being nervous with *me*?"

Not much she wasn't. Only as nervous as twelve cats with nervous breakdowns, though she certainly was hiding it well at the moment. Her voice was just a mumble. Believe me, that girl's bird's-eye view of life was undergoing a drastic change, even if she wouldn't get in the car just for a minute or two as he wanted, naturally. While he told her some more about art galleries, I imagine.

Maybe she was even playing her own little tease game. It's a marvel how these batty babes catch on when they're so minded. Finally she really began to tear herself away, so I gave Francis a pat and went sneaking back through the cars into the joint ahead of her.

A new face had been added. Sally's boyfriend Raymie was now a member of the merry group of revelers. I must say that neither old Asher nor Sally looked a bit happy about it.

Raymie was a dark slouchy guy with a long nose; he was a kind you would never expect to fasten their overshoes, if they ever wore them, but I saw Raymie on the street in town once, and he not only had them on, but they were zipped as neat as a preacher's. Furthermore, he had on an overcoat and a snapbrim hat, and I was amazed to see he wasn't half bad-looking.

Tonight, though, he needed a shave and wore dungarees and a faded-out shirt. I think he was driving a pulp truck, but as he never seemed to stay long at one job, I may be wrong. Quite often in the fall, he went to Aroostook County, Maine, to pick up potatoes; then he worked in a blueberry factory once, he told me. Also, during deer season one fall, he got out of a car with his gun cocked some way, and shot himself in the stomach. The doctors told him no one could do it again in a million years and live through it, which I guess was right.

When he got lit, which was not infrequent, as you may imagine, being the type he was, he always got hipped about that accident. It was a real obsession. "Just missed my God-damn liver," he would say in great amazement, over and over. "Would you believe how that Christly shot could of got me in the belly and missed my God-damn liver!"

When I arrived, Raymie and Emile were just starting the floor show. For a minute I thought they were just dancing together, which was a weird enough sight in itself, but that was not all. Raymie had a stub of cigarette in his mouth, and all of a sudden he flipped it over with his tongue, so the burning end was inside, and Emile put his old face down, being about two feet taller, and took it into *his* mouth, just with his lips. No hands.

What a pair of clowns. They really were a nauseating sight, but still it had a kind of horrid fascination. Around and around they kept dancing, as though they were made for each other, first Emile leading and then Raymie.

Emile was still in his dirty apron, and you might find it hard to picture, but he was very light on his feet, all five hundred pounds. Fat people are always good dancers for some odd reason.

Then Emile flipped the cigarette over with his lips, so the burning part was inside his mouth, and Raymie grabbed it back. The butt was beginning to look shopworn but they were still going strong.

Everyone gathered around to watch, naturally, laughing and making cracks, and they got fancier and fancier, with the butt going back and forth without a pause for breath, and all the time they never missed a beat, either of them. It was actually pretty clever. If they hadn't been two nutty guys you knew, in ordinary clothes, you might have thought they were doing a crazy jungle dance from darkest Africa.

Asher began shouting at them to stop. From his expression, he preferred Astaire and Kelly.

Sally was way over in the corner, staring into space. You can't really stare into space in just that fashion unless you're Sally, two-thirds lit. All at the same time she conveyed that she was bored to tears by the demonstration, that she was mad as a she-bear at Raymie, and that if anyone but a member of the opposite sex came near her she would spit flaming brimstone. Also, that if approached in the right way by same, she could be instantly persuaded into the bedroom. Sally was quite a woman in her own simple way.

Someone pulled my arm and there was Susan, with a look of utmost horror. "Oh, come *on*," she said. "I want to go *home*." Actually she was a little green. She couldn't watch them and she couldn't look away, like a mesmerized hen.

In my opinion it was silly to back out at that point with a mouth-watering steak practically on our plates, but she certainly wasn't kidding about being upset. Anyhow, this farce had gone on long enough. In a situation like that, there's just one thing to do: Take action! So I grabbed Raymie's shirttail and held on.

"You're nauseating the customers," I said. "Where you two ought to be is a sideshow, between the two-headed baby and the bearded woman!"

Emile bristled like jelly, quivering in every pore, and started to scream abuse, but Raymie was ready for a change and flung his arms around me, tickled blue at being insulted. "My old friend, Evelyn! Where you *been*, honey chile?" Over his shoulder to Emile, he said, "Shut up, you old tub; didn't you hear what the lady said?"

"When are we going to eat?" I inquired, ignoring Emile's remarks, and Asher started hissing like a time fuse, remembering how hungry he was.

"Get h'out to the kitchen, fat slob, you. We've got h'invited guests. What you think, we run a music 'all?" He looked very menacing as well as comical, and Emile went. Food meant more to him than any other pastime.

Fortunately, a joker I hadn't even noticed before asked Susan to dance, a fatherly-looking creep with a paunch, but not awfully old, I guess.

So Raymie and I settled down for a quiet chat.

"I'm getting God-damn sick and tired of this run-around," he said, right away. I don't know why people always think I long to hear their troubles. I must look sympathetic or something. "Chris' sake, Evelyn, you know they don't want me in here a-*tall*?

Sally give me orders to wait outside nights till she gets through work. Chris' sake! Do I look stupid or something?"

"She's just trying to feather your nest, Raymie," I said, soothingly.

"You're God-damn right, kid. And what'll she ever get out of that old bag of wind?" He gave a big hoot. "Anyways, kid, it's more fun than a circus. Stick around and watch me rile 'em up! For two cents the old goat would call George and have me heaved out of here."

George was a state cop, but nobody paid much attention to that because they knew him. Probably a stranger spotting STATE POLICE across the back of his Ford might think he looked real tough, especially as he was a beefy guy around the ears, but George was really about as tough as a piece of toilet paper.

In connection with George, I have a very vivid recollection. I guess it's one of those memories that will stick with you till death, for no reason in particular, except at the time I was pretty kiddish and it made a deep impression. George was older than me, by six or seven years, and so was this other crumb, Albion, but being neighborhood kids, I sometimes tagged around behind them. This particular day we were hanging around Albion's backyard, I don't recall what-doing or anything, but Albion was fooling with his father's hammer and all of a sudden he held it up above George's head and just let it drop. The clunk is what I remember, just the dull old clunk on George's head, and being so little, I right away felt sick, because I knew he shouldn't have done a thing like that.

But George just sort of grinned and rubbed his skull, and didn't even hit him back. He never was a ball of fire in the mental department, but every time I think of that clunk I have the same sicky feeling. It happened so easy and yet you couldn't ever take it back.

Albion was the same kid who, a little later in life, kept trying to get me behind the big willow tree in our yard to see the difference between little boys and little girls. Boys are very naive bastards at times.

He was the only dirty kid around—unwashed, I mean—which put him in a sort of special category, and also around that same time he was making dreadful faces in school, not on purpose but as though his face itched. The school nurse said it was nerves. Probably caused by not being able to persuade any girls to go behind trees with him for an illustrated lecture.

Albion may have been cut out for a professor, you can't tell, and we were thwarting his instincts. As a matter of fact, the professors I've happened to run across all seem pretty hipped on sex and so on, so Albion would have fitted right in. Of course I don't mean the old ones; they act more like ministers.

Sally had left off staring into space. She was staring at us.

"Honey," I said to Raymie, displaying some affection especially for her benefit, as she might as well have something on her mind as nothing, "your better half is seeing red."

"First she's mad 'cause I come in, then she's mad 'cause I'm enjoying myself," he said, in great good humor. "She knows what she can do. God, she's drunk as an owl. I just danced with Aunty to get her goat."

Just then I actually smelled steak frying. It put six months on my life expectancy.

Emile had fastened the door back so he could get dinner and watch too.

We started dancing again and I twined my arm around Raymie's neck as though he was strictly my idea of heaven. He was still confiding his troubles, but they didn't dampen his spirits much.

"It's got so I have to drink just outta self-defense. I tell you, Evelyn, maybe you don't realize it, but when one party's drunk and the other ain't, it's no soap unless you got no feelings. Maybe most people don't know it about me, but I'm a pretty sensitive guy. I got feelings. I tell you, kid, it gets me down having her come at me with that look in her eye. And you know for all the hell she cares, it could be ten other guys, depending if they was handy. When she's boiled, I mean. When I'm boiled too, who gives a damn? Hey, kid! That's life, ain't it!"

Baring his soul like that made him thirsty, so we went back to the table.

Susan and Mr. Front Porch were getting along fine, but she was still uneasy and kept giving me looks. While we were dancing, I could hear him telling her how surprised he was to find her in a place like that, knowing what a nice girl and so forth she was. It turned out he was the meter man who came every month and read the electric meter at the house and also old Livewire's at the barbershop.

Uncle Becker's bill certainly never caused the electric company to turn handsprings. If it was pitch-dark he'd never think it was worth all the trouble to get up to turn on a light. Anyway, it might attract customers. A lot of times in the winter I'd stop there in the late afternoon just to see what he would do. Every other store along the street would be lighted and anyone might think his place was closed up, but oh no, he would be sitting right in there smoking his pipe. So I'd go in and slam the door to make sure he was awake and say, "How about a piece of candy, Mr. Becker?"

After a few grunts and groans he would say, "Well, I s'pose that means we got to turn on the lights. On the wall there. You can reach it easier'n I can."

The switch turned on both lights, one over the candy counter, which was about fifteen watts, and one over the barber chair, which might have been thirty. After I bought a penny piece of candy I always waited for the next move, which I knew by heart. The thing was, Mr. Becker would never be bothered to turn the lights off again as long as someone had turned them on for him, the switch being as much as ten feet away, but he took a rickety old stool he had, one of them about as shaky as the other, and climbed up and unscrewed the bulb over the barber chair. It must have saved him as much as two cents a week, but you could see that foxing the Hydro-Electric gave him a lot of satisfaction.

Anyhow, the meter man had a father complex along with bad posture, which may have been caused by flat feet, running from house to house every month, and he was real concerned about

Susan, which relieved her mind so much she began to feel like a woman of the world and almost enjoy herself.

Sally began to hoist sail, so I left Raymie at the table, figuring he was a better sailor than I was, and also had got mixed up with her of his own free will.

"Emile, you're making a wonderful stink," I said. As long as our life depended on food and our food on him, there was no sense biting the wrong hand.

He just grunted and kept on standing in the doorway, slapping a spatula against his stomach. Old Asher was slumped down behind the cash register having a snooze. He looked pathetic and shriveled up, and he'd gone to sleep with his mouth open.

"That bitch of a Sally," I said, to reestablish a friendly footing, "why doesn't she let the old boy alone? Raymie'll give her the boot if she's not careful."

"Uh! That woman!" he said, waving his spatula. "She's dirt. She's got no *char*acter, whatsoever, Evelyn."

"Brother, you're not kidding," I agreed. "How long'll it be before we eat?"

"Maybe twenty minutes." He gave me a real blank stare with those little slits of his. "You may be interested to know it's western steer beef, the *best* there is."

"Oh brother," I said. "It smells de-lumptious, Emile."

He was staring over my shoulder. "Little tart," he hissed. "That woman don't own one shred of common decency to her name."

I turned around. Sally reminded me of a big spider hustling away with a little black fly, except Raymie was really as big as she was. He was fluttering his wings and struggling, but in her present state she could have subdued Tarzan, and they disappeared toward the back.

No one paid much attention to the abduction. Probably most of those characters would have kept right on dancing if Little Red Riding Hood had shot in the door with the wolf on her tail. Except possibly Jonas. He was always interested in a new female. But at present Luella had him tied up in knots. They were leaning across the table like a couple of nearsighted owls telling each other their life secrets. That conversation should have been recorded for posterity. Probably in a couple of hundred years they would have had it in the Library of Congress as a valuable document to explain all the rapes and murders of the twentieth century.

Susie and her Knight of the Meter Boxes were also sitting it out, getting acquainted. However, I doubt this conversation would have explained anything.

"Emile," I said, "you think we ought to go see what Sally's up to? Maybe they're stealing the plumbing fixtures or something."

Emile looked radiant at the idea. "Oh my yes, Evelyn. You're in*spir*ed, dear. Absolutely, yes. Let's go and see."

"Well, check on the steak first," I said.

We went sneaking down the hall together, with Emile exploding like a warm pop bottle, with the giggles. Outside Sally's door we waited a minute or two making sure they were in there, and then Emile burst the door open with a really insane shriek of laughter.

"What you *doing*, you little sneaks?" He was hardly able to control himself, being his idea of mad fun. All in all it was a pretty crummy idea. . . .

Raymie came bouncing to the door, as hepped up as Emile. I wouldn't have blamed him for being riled, but no, he thought it was hilarious too. Old Sally had grabbed a blanket up around her shoulders and believe me, I never saw a woman so unamused by anything. Not that I really blamed her.

"Naughty, naughty," Emile bawled. "What you doing in here? Naughty, naughty!"

"You damn nosy pansy, what you *think*?" Sally shouted. "It any of *your* business?"

Right here I will explain that some of the language that was used, I've been told—but not by any authority that amounts to much—had better be left out. This authority said that my command of the English language throughout was not spectacular and that I needn't worry that anybody would have trouble ciphering out the meaning, even a two-year-old. There's a large tinge of sour grapes to all that, but just in passing let me say that on Susan's account, in case she should ever read this, I am very glad to leave some words out. If so, I hope she will accept this gesture in the spirit it was intended.

This authority abovementioned also remarked, Did I think I was Hemingway or something, which didn't mean that he was asking a question, only grabbing an opportunity to throw names around, which he dearly loves more than food and drink. I can only say that if there's one thing I do happen to know, it's who I am.

Raymie was hopping around, howling like a loon and holding his stomach, as though this was the funniest moment, bar none, that ever came his way.

But Sally and Emile were swapping colorful samples of their vocabulary back and forth and it didn't sound like fooling. Then Sally sat straight up, forgetting all about the blanket, leaving modesty to the winds—though with Sally that may not be the right term, as I imagine she left that to the winds a long time ago—and began to grab anything she could reach to throw at us. She had pretty good aim too. I know what they mean by a hail of fire: old beer bottles, ashtrays mostly full, a *True Detective* magazine, a bottle of Vick's VapoRub, and a plate with a moldy ham sandwich on it which hit Emile square in the nose.

This enraged him. It didn't take much doing even under normal circumstances. He got very red and convulsed-looking and began squealing like a pig with the stomachache, and then *he* began gathering up an armload of ammunition too. A few shoes and a handbag lying on a chair, everything on the bureau, cold-cream jars, hand lotion, cologne bottles, a box of Kleenex, and an open carton of cigarettes that flew in all directions. When he picked up the lamp which was pretty big, I decided no one would miss me.

Sally charged off the bed like a catapult, just in her slip, but brother, she didn't need any coat of mail. Raymie had ducked into a foxhole behind a chair, still thinking it was a big joke. I admired his sense of humor, but give me a seat in the balcony.

I scooted out of there and up the hall like a cockroach with something biting it. There was one thought in my head: to scram out of Asher's Bar and Grill but fast. Leave them to their little pleasures, such as killing each other; it was high time for us to be home in bed. Actually, we were pretty young to be fooling around with their age group.

But at the kitchen door the smell of that steak brought me up short. Holy Mother, I thought, it'll be ruined. I better turn it off or something. It was done right then, all brown and dripping and gorgeous, and pushing it off the burner as my good deed of the day, the thought occurred that I might just take a snack along to soothe our hungry little tummies after we got home. It certainly wouldn't be mooching. We'd been invited for a meal.

Old Asher was still hunched over the cash register, snoring through his nose, and by a remarkable coincidence the jukebox was playing a Spike Jones record. Otherwise you would certainly have heard the commotion down yonder, where they seemed to be breaking up the furniture and throwing it at each other. As it was, the yowls fitted right into the orchestra music. Spike should have hired that trio. He wouldn't have had to do another lick of work himself.

Anyhow, there was no time for idle speculation, so I took a quick peek in the refrigerator. It was pretty disgusting: a lot of hot dogs, raw naturally, and hamburger patties, likewise, and a bushel or so of lettuce. My saliva doesn't start churning at the sight of a lettuce leaf, even on the point of collapse. Emile had also gone overboard on artichokes. They were all over the place, whole and partly pruned. He probably gorged himself on them. Just his speed. Personally, by the time I get to the part that's worth it, I'm tired of the whole idea.

Like one day when my mother was too busy to pick the meat out of the lobsters, like she always did, and put them right on the table whole, the way they do in restaurants.

Dad took one look at the platter and began to swear.

"For Christ's sake," he said, "when I sit down to the table I want to eat my dinner, not wrestle with it."

I did finally see some dill pickles and a big bowl of potato salad. He had about a gallon of those old black olives, with pits to break your teeth on, which I intensely dislike. Old lady Ogden is another one who couldn't survive a day without black olives full of pits. Artichokes, too, are one of her big delights. "Oh my *dear* Mr. Tucker, no *artichokes*! How will I dare to *face* my husband!"

How Emile kept up the farce of feeding the public with that collection was beyond me. There was an old ham butt and salami and stuff like that; also Velveeta cheese, which I took a package of, in case of extreme necessity.

But it suddenly came to me that I was mad poking around the leftovers and leaving that steak just *sitting* there. How stupid can you be?

Those happy people in the bedroom probably wouldn't be able to crawl, let alone eat, and poor old Mr. Asher was sitting out there longing for nothing but his bed. Food was very bad for elderly people at night, anybody knew that. Steak would only upset his digestion. It might bring on a fatal heart attack, and poor old pirate, he had trouble enough about to fall on his head from the boys in the back room, let alone a heart seizure.

It would really make things much simpler if I just took the steak along with Susan and me and then no one had to worry about its going to waste. My mother brought me up to avoid waste, in any disguise.

All this meditation in actual time took very little, and I had the dill pickles already in my pocket, plus a big plastic bag full of salad, the bag the ham had been in, also a salt shaker and the Velveeta. The box of waxed paper was stuck way up on top of a cupboard. Emile could reach it, I suppose, being ten feet tall, but glory be, I had to drag over a chair. But I had to wrap the steak in *something*.

By this time I was in a nervous sweat, and threatened with hysterics at how comical the whole episode was, all the time hearing the howls and bangs from down the hall and the howls and bangs and toots from Spike Jones, and scared to death someone would appear from one direction or the other and catch me. Not that I felt especially guilty, just that I was too tired to cope with any more colorful personalities. All I wanted was to drive peacefully home to Susan's and have a quiet repast of steak in the seclusion of her room, with no one to bother, and then sleep, lovely glorious sleep. I was ready to sleep for a week.

The dust was an inch thick on top of that cupboard. It was too high for anyone to bother about, even Emile couldn't see up there, though he must have been able to reach. And speaking of surprises, someone had stowed a jar of Swift's peanut butter way back against the wall, behind the wax paper. It was a pretty peculiar place for peanut butter, even granting the well-known peculiarity around here, so I gave an extra grunt but couldn't reach the damn thing. I had to get down and grab a long fork thing and climb up there again, by this time really sweating blood.

I finally fished it where I could reach. The top was rusted, showing it must have been there a long time, and—take a grip on yourself—inside under a dried-up slice of bologna that nearly finished me, just the smell, was a roll of absolute money. Real as real!

I was spellbound. In fact, I was so amazed that I stuck the bologna back in, screwed on the top, and pushed it back out of sight as though it burned my fingers, not even having touched it.

I hope anyone who up to now has jumped to any conclusions, not having bothered to read this complete story, but jumping here and there for shock treatment, sex, and swear words, will note the above fact and calm down. I'm just as honest as you are, my friend, and maybe a trifle more so. Anyhow, I tore off a piece of waxed paper, got it around the steak, burned my fingers, finally got a wad of napkins outside the paper, and stuffed it all into my pocket, getting more panicky by the minute. Old Father Time had been playing my way but he was a changeable old bastard.

I managed to slow down to a fast walk going into the bar after Susan, with the steak burning a hole through my intestines, and an insane desire to sit down and howl with laughter in everybody's face, but most of all, a big urge to get the hell out of there. Susan was sitting at the end of the bar all by herself, through some luck too fortunate to mention, as Mr. Meter was out attending to a meter, and of all times and places she was scribbling away on a napkin. But I couldn't wait on the muse at that point.

"Let's shove, screwball," I said. "And fast."

She looked startled but willing. In fact, pleased as a pup, having wanted to go for hours. So we walked out, no trouble at all, looking highly inconspicuous. Jonas didn't even notice, being pretty glazed himself by that time.

Francis responded to my touch like a real gentleman and we wasted no futile time in warming up but tore out of Asher's Bar and Grill at top speed. A Cadillac might have had more power, but no more spirit.

Susan lay back yawning and it never occurred to her that we were making a getaway. Of course, I often decide to leave a place very spur of the moment, so she was used to it. Anyway, she was so glad to be going home it was pathetic. Believe me, I wouldn't have stuck around five minutes if I'd wanted out that much. But that was Susan. I guess she figured if she didn't know *what* she wanted, how could she be sure what she didn't want? Of course, it had been a pretty strenuous evening for her, having to cope with a man. In fact, when I thought it over, old Susie had done surprising. Dancing with Jonas, even latching onto Mr. Meter as a last gasp. Our girl was definitely showing signs of life. I was pleased, but not too much. It wouldn't be right somehow for Susie to start acting like everybody else.

I guess I needn't have worried though. That would have been the trick to stump the experts.

The Meter Man's name was Mr. Brimmer, and he sounded like one long tale of woe. The type of man who yaks about his wife all the time strikes me as a real drool. His wife had a sluggish colon and caught athlete's foot while in the hospital. And his son had to have shots in the tail every week for being allergic to breathing, which cost five bucks a jolt. Mother of men! The spark of life in some people is certainly no bonfire.

"Gosh, I'm so *tired*." She sounded pretty happy, as though we'd come to the end of a perfect day.

"For crying out loud, Sue," I said, "don't you know what a sluggish colon is?"

"Well, what is it?"

"It's being constipated, you dope!"

That put us in good humor, and Francis went skipping along like a child again.

The nice cool air poured in, and the frogs were kerchunking way off somewhere, and no one in the world was on the road but us. We sang "Heart of My Heart" and "The Rose of Tralee" at the top of our lungs all the way home, with Susie taking the alto on the last note. That was the only time she could ever hit it, on the very last note.

"Maybe I'll stay all night at your house," I said. "Okay?" I did that fairly often when we were out late together.

"Oh *sure*." She was delighted, naturally. Sometimes it touched my conscience having her so pleased about little things like that.

We tiptoed in very quietly and she locked the door. I thought of suggesting that we get a knife and plates and so on, but it seemed too much trouble and we started upstairs, holding on to each other to keep from giggling, and not putting any lights on.

But Mrs. Becker heard us. She always did. "Is that you, Susan?"

"Yes, Aunt Clara. It's me and Evelyn. I'm sorry we woke you up."

"It's *very* late, Susan. I can't think why you stayed out so late. Didn't you know how worried I'd be?"

"Oh gosh, Aunt Clara, I'm sorry. You shouldn't have worried. Honest. We went to a couple of movies."

"Well, get right to bed, then, and don't talk half the night," she said. "Get Evelyn a clean towel."

Even when Mrs. Becker sounded cross, which she often did at a time like that when she had probably been lying awake for hours wondering where Susan was, and not being very reassured to know she was under my rattle-brained wing, I never minded what she said. I mean, I never blamed her. It's a funny thing, but I really *liked* Mrs. Becker more than anyone else around. I don't know why, because in my whole life I never said much to her except, "It's a nice day, Mrs. Becker," or "Thanks for sending me a jelly tart, Mrs. Becker," but that's the way it was.

Most people I didn't think much about one way or another, as far as liking them went. I mean, there they were, either pretty crummy or pretty dumb or odd Mauds or full of high purpose and low practice or whatever their line happened to be, and I took them as they came, being all human beings, roughly, and interesting from that standpoint. But Mrs. Becker, though she would probably die to know it, occupied a very special place in my acquaintanceship.

When we were in Susie's room with the door shut, I went over to the little table she used for a desk and began to clear everything off it.

"What's the matter?" She thought I'd gone slightly cuckoo.

Then I pulled out the bag of potato salad, which was pretty mashed but not hurt any, and the dill pickles and the package of Velveeta. She began to giggle, and the more I pulled out, the more hysterical she got, until she had to poke her head into a pillow.

"Wait, looney," I said. "You don't even know the best."

How I ever got that steak crammed inside my pocket, I'll never know, because we had an awful time getting it out. I had to take the jacket off and she held one side while I pulled on the other. We got so weak that we couldn't stand up, and the darned thing finally popped out on the bed between us. We didn't have anything but fingers to eat with, but who cared. First she took a big bite and then I did, getting juice all over our faces and hands, and then taking a spoonful of potato salad. She found a spoon in the bathroom. Believe me, food never tasted so good. We really took our time and relished that meal. The cheese we finally ate for dessert.

By that time we were so stuffed and messy and greasy and tired, all we could do was sit on the bed and look at each other and die. I don't think either of us ever felt so good or so sort of close and satisfied and pooped. As Charlie was fond of saying, it was a real big deal.

Then Mrs. Becker rapped on the door. She was standing there in a faded pink bathrobe she always wore, with a big shawl collar and with her hair hanging down her back in two stringy braids like a little girl's. Her face looked very small and shrunken, as she had taken out her dental plates hours ago.

"What *are* you girls doing?" she said, but the wonderful thing about Mrs. Becker, even though she was so cross right then, when she got a good look at us she had to smile. "Bless me, you'll be my death. Eating at this time of night. *Why* didn't you go down in the kitchen—well, that's spilled milk. Now run along and wash up, Evelyn. Come now, it's high time you were both in bed. Look at this mess, Susan. Well, you'll just have it to clean up in the morning. The whole room needs a scrubbing, mind. Floor and all."

"Yes, Aunt Clara," Susan said. "I'll do it myself. First thing. We didn't mean to keep you up."

"No more nonsense, now," she said, "or you won't be able to have friends stay after this. It's a blessed wonder you haven't waked your uncle."

I didn't take long in the bathroom, not blaming her for being peeved. It was real late. I made Susan hurry too. Naturally she undressed in there for reasons of personal modesty, and while I was lying in bed in a pair of her pajamas waiting for her, I thought about Mrs. Becker and Uncle Becker. How she ever put up with that excuse for flies to light on was beyond me.

I knew of only one time when she was really provoked and couldn't help showing it. Naturally old Becker never worked up the energy to paint anything, inside or out, and the barbershop got dingier and dingier every summer. But the old pickle wouldn't hear of its being painted, even when *she* wanted to have it done and pay for it out of the boarders. He was born stubborn. Let someone want him to get up and his backside was cemented to the chair. Which it was by natural function anyway. One summer, though, she couldn't stand it any longer, and she hired a painter to go ahead and paint it white.

Old Becker sat there in the window for two weeks watching the painter paint, and when he made an extra big effort and put an expression on his face, it wasn't happy. I guess he felt slightly embarrassed because everyone knew his wife was paying for it. When the painter got to the big windows in front, he came in and said, "What color trim your wife want on these windows, or don't she want any?"

Old Becker didn't even turn around. "Suit yourself," he said. "I don't know nothing whatever about it." Using all that breath probably tired him out for the day.

"I better go see Mrs. Becker then and find out."

"She ain't to home," the old weasel said. He knew where she was, right down the street in the Church vestry at the meeting of the Women's Society for Christian Service, tying a quilt. "Go ahead and suit yourself," he said, and tipped back in his chair and went to sleep.

As Dad said, everybody that knew Farley, the painter, knew he'd paint the trim either orange or black if it was up to him, whereas anybody who looked at Mrs. Becker's house could see she had painted the trim white like the rest of the house. Probably Mr. Becker had never noticed. It would have meant raising his eyes.

So Farley went out and painted the trim around the windows orange, bright orange. It took him all the afternoon. At four o'clock all the Christian women came chirping out of the vestry and up the street right past the barbershop. Farley had gone home by then. He worked from seven to eleven and from twelve to four, which meant leaving off by three-thirty.

Mrs. Becker came along with the others and long before she got there she spotted the trim. It really made a showing. Of course, people like Farley thought it was a knock-out. It was all a matter of taste, but Mrs. Becker was paying for it. She walked right into the barbershop and never said a word. Just stood there looking at Uncle Trouble. Someone who just happened to be there said her eyes were brimming, she felt so bad.

"Albert, how could you let that man do it?"

"Do what, Clara?"

"Paint that *hideous* color around the windows."

"Why, I must have been busy with a customer. Don't it suit?"

"It *ruins* the whole building." Her voice was trembling, the best she could do. "Oh, Albert, I thought you understood that I *did not* want a color on the trim."

"Lord, I had the business in here to tend to. I couldn't watch his every move, Clara. Anyway, I don't see as it makes so much difference."

She turned and went out without another word. Old Becker picked up his fly swatter and actually looked around for a fly, without waiting for it to light on him. He must have been really keyed up.

Susan and I were so tired we couldn't go right to sleep. So I started telling her how Charlie and I were washed up, finished positively.

"That's what you say now."

We were whispering under the covers so Mrs. Becker wouldn't hear.

"That adolescent!" I whispered back. "You'll see, Susie. He's just someone I used to know. Where do you suppose we'll all be this time next year?"

That was a sobering thought, and we lay in the dark feeling very prophetic and sentimental about the past, and also plenty worried.

I rolled over and put my arm around her. She felt very skinny and it really gave me a pang thinking of her having to battle the stinkpots of this world. Especially with her drawbacks.

"Listen," I said, "no matter what, no matter where we are or what we're doing, we'll be like right now. We'll always keep in touch, Susie. Isn't that right?"

"Oh golly," she said. "Yes."

"There's just one thing, dear," I said. "About Hine. Sue, for God's sake, don't let him fool around just because you think it's time you did or something. Honest, that guy is poison. I got a clairvoyant feeling he's not your type. There's plenty of other guys."

She began to shake, and rolled over so I couldn't tell for a minute whether she was laughing or crying.

"Honey, what's the matter?"

Then I knew she was laughing. "Oh you big droop," I said. "What's so funny, I'd like to inquire?"

"You," she gurgled. "You've had him on the brain all day." She flopped over again, still shaking. "You sound . . . you sound like you're jealous, Evelyn!" Then she went off into another gale.

That really rocked me. And lying there thinking it over, I realized it might be true. Maybe I was old Mother Screwball herself, and didn't know it.

"You're real gone," I said. "You give me the twitters. I should be jealous of that little monster, for the love of Pete! Take him, go play house with him, I should care less, except for your sake."

"Okay, okay." She wasn't taken down a bit. In fact, she kept on chuckling for quite a while into my shoulder.

Downstairs a clock struck and I tried to count. "What time is it, anyhow?"

"Later than you think," she said, and went off again.

"You're getting hysterical," I said, shaking her. "Now listen, we got to get to sleep. You go ahead while I have my thought for the day."

All of a sudden she lay very still. "Just tell me something first," she whispered.

"What, for the love of Mike? Gee whiz, you're changeable tonight."

"Just . . . just have you . . . I mean, were you . . . I mean, did you . . . did you ever . . . you know . . . with Charlie?"

For a minute I didn't answer. Then I said, "Yes."

She didn't say anything, just lay there perfectly still, like a warm stone.

"You mean you want to know what it's like, Sue?" She just nodded a little, never moving. This was a very serious moment and I knew it. To even have her ask was strictly unbelievable. I wanted to say just the right thing, but for once in my life I was really low on gas. I mean, it was a pretty responsible position, and all of a sudden I felt like a mother hen with a chicken who only understood Russian.

Finally I said, "Well, dear, it's, it's wonderful when you want it. I mean, don't *do* it unless you want to. Then it's . . . it's . . . well, I mean you can't really say. It's sort of . . . sort of . . . well, I mean, just wonderful, and you can't bear it, you want him to so much."

To my amazement, I was very embarrassed, so to ease the tension I gave her a shake and said, "For God's sake, don't do it just because you're curious. Wait till the right moment comes along. Otherwise, it would be very awkward afterward and you'd probably kill yourself. Now, let's go to sleep."

"All right," she said, and actually she sounded perfectly normal, not a bit upset. In fact, capable of making a crack. "You're about as articulate as a deaf-mute!"

"Oh, is that so?"

"It sure is," she said, chuckling and yawning. "Stop and listen to yourself sometime."

I pinched her until she took it back and then we went to sleep.

Part IV

After Midnight

It must have been about half-past two or so in the morning when somebody began to pound on the door. There's bound to be something pretty awful the matter when anyone has the nerve to do that, with the whole town dark and peaceful and quiet. And this wasn't any restrained knock, it was a sudden, God-awful racket.

We both woke up in about one instant. In fact, I was sitting straight up in bed before I really knew I was awake, trying to decide if it was a thunderstorm or what.

Then we realized it was someone downstairs at the front door. Susan began to shiver like a nervous spaniel. "Wh . . . what d-do you suppose is the matter?"

"Don't get so excited," I said. "The house is probably on fire."

She managed to chuckle. "I don't smell any smoke."

That settled the question of fire, because if someone forty miles away blew out a match she could smell the sulphur. I never knew any person—bar none—with a nose like hers, and it was always smoke or scorching hair, smells like that, that Calamity Jane never missed a whiff of.

Across the hall Mrs. Becker was trying to bring Uncle Wildfire to life, and to my surprise she finally did. He went padding around in his bare feet for a few minutes working up pressure and finally got a window open.

"What's wanted?" he called down.

Their room was above the front door and Susan's was in the back, so we couldn't hear what was said, but the window banged down and Uncle Becker went charging downstairs with his pants pulled on over his nightshirt. Mrs. Becker went down too, pretty slow, holding onto her faded old bathrobe and trying to keep her slippers on, looking very shrunken and harried.

I had the door ajar peeking out while Susan lay in bed shivering, but we weren't in mystery long. Mrs. Becker came to get us.

"They want you two girls." I was afraid she might collapse, she looked so sick and worried. "Oh dear, what have you got mixed up in, Evelyn? It's the police. It's George Cotton and another man and they want you. Oh tell me, for mercies' sake, what you've done."

Susan was as white as a ghost. But she never went down in a pinch, I must say. "We haven't d-done anything, Aunt Clara, honest, that's the truth. They . . . they've made a mistake."

I wanted to hug her, big eyes and all, because God Almighty, I wasn't near as positive as that. My mind was racing back and forth over that nutty night like a squirrel, and for an awful moment I thought maybe I'd poked that roll of dough in my pocket, just as a nervous reflex, and they were here to get it back. Or maybe Emile had conked old Sally with the lamp or vice versa and they were trying to ring me in. One thing I could swear to till my dying day, I hadn't hit anyone with anything, not even a bobby pin. Just an innocent bystander. Bystander, anyway. When I got that settled with myself, my brain began to stop giving off sparks, but, believe me, I was getting a little shaky too, strictly from excitement. Having no classy kimono handy, I got into my pedal-pushers in nothing flat while Mrs. Becker stewed, and Susan managed to take off her pajamas and get dressed right in front of me. The lash of necessity or something.

Downstairs, George and another state cop and Uncle Becker were standing in the hall looking grim. At least the cops looked grim. Uncle Becker looked sleepy. Apparently he hadn't worked himself up to asking them any questions. It was only his own niece they were after.

"You girls in to Asher's Bar and Grill tonight?" George said, very professionally. Not even a hello, though he did sort of nod first. I was tempted to say, "Listen, punk, pull that act with some other girl," but on Mrs. Becker's account, held myself in. Also I was still poking furtively through my pockets for incriminating evidence.

"Sure we were," I said. "It's a free country."

"Somebody's bumped the old man off," George said.

Mrs. Becker gave a little moan and grabbed Mr. Becker's arm.

I couldn't believe he had really said it. In fact, for a minute the whole thing seemed like something I must have dreamed up from indigestion, us standing there at the door, shivering, and not even awake, with Mrs. Becker looking about to faint, old Becker with his mouth open, and George and his pal just staring at us, like they had taken root.

But it didn't go away and I didn't wake up. We just went right on standing there, with the cold air coming in. Then I began to be scared. Usually even when I'm scared, one part of my head keeps on being sort of fascinated by what's going on, but not this time. All I could think of was how I wished I was home in my mother's bed.

"Yeh," the other cop said, with a fishy stare at Susan and me. "That's the story. He was found with his skull bashed in. About an hour ago. George saw your car up there pretty late last night, so you girls can help us a lot by cooperating. Tell us who was there, what was said, everything you remember, whatever you know."

"How can they know anything?" Mrs. Becker cried. She might be practically dying of shock, but she wasn't going down without a fight. The way she took it on the chin right then made me feel even worse, except that was impossible. There wasn't room.

"What can they know about murder?" Her eyes looked like shiny brown scared horse chestnuts. "Oh mercy, mercy. My niece has *never* been mixed up with such people."

"Sure, sure, that's right, Mrs. Becker," George said. "Only they was there tonight. I *know* that. And there's damned little else we do know. So they can maybe help us out a lot, see? It's just for questioning we want to take them. We know they got nothing to do with it, but maybe they can give us a steer."

"Take them! Susan is certainly not going back to that place. I won't allow it. She's just a child. I won't have it. Albert, put your foot down. Susan is not to leave this house."

I felt sick at my stomach. It was a mess any way you looked at it. Personally, I didn't want to look. Old Mr. Asher snoozing away behind his cash register with his glasses falling off.

"Look George," I said, trying not to gag, "I'll go with you. She wouldn't know anything anyhow."

The other cop was older than George and taller. He wore rimless glasses.

"This girl was there with you, wasn't she?" he said to me. "You were both there tonight, together?"

"Well, yes," I said, "but she doesn't know any of those clowns. She couldn't help a bit. Why don't you leave her alone?"

"Look sister," he said. "We got no time to play games. You was both there. So you both come along with us now. She looks to me like she had eyes in her head, just the same as you."

Yes, but she doesn't see as much with them. Only I said that to myself. What's the use of arguing with a big dumb buster in a uniform? Put a man in a garbage-collector's suit and he feels real keen, distinguished from the poor old general public.

Looking him over revived me a little. Having the door open helped too. The cold night air was just what I needed.

"Then I insist on going with her," Mrs. Becker said. She looked so little in that loose old bathrobe, and her eyes were so wild and dark with those kid braids hanging down her back that I wished some way I could tell her not to worry. A lot of good it would have done.

"You'll have to wait while I dress myself," she said.

"We've wasted time already," the fishy-eyed cop said. "I got daughters of my own, ma'am. Nothing's going to happen to her."

"But she's just a school girl. How can she possibly be any help to you?"

The cop took Susan's arm and started out. She was so stunned, horrified, scared, embarrassed, and a few other things, that I don't think she could have told them who she was, but as far as they were concerned she was going to put the finger right on Mr. Murderer.

"It's my opinion they grow up pretty fast," he said to Mrs. Becker. "If they was old enough to spend the evening dancing in a cheap beer parlor, I guess they can stand answering a few questions."

"Albert! If they won't have me, you'll have to go with her."

Oh brother! If I hadn't been generally overcome, that would have given me hysterics.

"Oh *no*, Aunt Clara!" Even Susan thought it was a weird suggestion.

To all intents and purposes Uncle Becker was back upstairs snug in his bed, though his eyes did blink once in a while. The biggest thing in life was getting his rest, and don't think I'm kidding. A little affair like murder couldn't hold up the program very long.

"Why Clara, what in the world could I do?" Actually he was a little nettled with her. "The girl'll be all right with George. All they want is to ask them questions. What good would it do for me to stay up?"

"That's right," George said, and nudged me out the door in front of him. "You got my word, Mrs. Becker. Don't you worry now."

He got in Francis with me, and Fish Eye took Susan in the police car. I suppose they were being real foxy so we couldn't fix up any stories between us, and also, they could try to worm out something on the way.

"You know who did it, George?" I said.

"Nope." He sat back like a ton of bricks expecting Francis to do all the work. Four or five of his cylinders were still asleep, too, and who could blame them at that ungodly hour. The air was so thin and pure and lonesome it made him wheeze. Francis was too old to have his sleep upset.

It was quite chilly, with white clouds of mist hanging across the low parts of the road.

"What's *your* idea?"

This was supposed to be flattery. The arm of the law hanging on little Evelyn's every word. Big deal.

"Poor old Mr. Asher," I said.

Then for a minute or two I couldn't say anything, or even see much. George pretended not to notice, and kept staring straight ahead.

When the fog lifted, I said, "How about Emile and Sally? Weren't they there when it happened?"

"Not a damn soul around. Some truck driver saw a light and stopped in to see what was up."

Now that I was wide awake, I stopped being so scared, mostly from amazement. Here were Francis and I lurching along the River Road up to Route 1 at three in the morning, with George Cotton lighting us both a cigarette. He smoked Chesterfields, thank God.

"Where . . . where was he?"

"In the middle of the floor. He's still there."

It was hard to tell whether George was really alive under all that paraphernalia, belts and holsters and badges and boots and stuff. But he wasn't a bad guy, either before or after he was beaned.

"God!" I said. "I wish I could help, George, but there isn't much I can think of. Except everybody was guzzling a lot of beer last night. When we left, Mr. Asher had gone to sleep behind the cash register."

"Well, tell Lieutenant Feeley anything you can."

"Lieutenant *Feeley*?" I said.

Even in the undone state I was in, that brought a spark of interest. I remembered seeing Lieutenant Feeley one night under very illuminating circumstances, though he didn't see me, or Charlie either. But that was long ago and far away and had nothing to do with now.

"Yeh, he's in charge. Step on it. How do you ever get this jalopy past inspection?"

The patrol car's lights kept winking out of sight ahead of us, with Francis complaining that he didn't care if he never caught up, and after that crack he almost went and sat in the ditch out of spite.

"Oh, I got friends," I said, and grinned at him with what *salut* I could scrape up. After all, he was one, too, from way back. "Remember when Albion dropped that hammer on your head?"

"Yeh, it still aches when I think of it." He grinned back and I stopped resenting his stiff britches. He had a sort of disarming grin. "Remember whether anybody up there seemed to be mad with Asher last night?"

"Well, honest to God, George, they were *all* mad last night."

Then it hit me that some crackpot had actually *done* it. Before, it was Mr. Asher I'd been thinking about. It was fortunate Francis knew the road so well because I was so bowled over I just gave him his head.

My mind began to spin like crazy, what this one said, what that one said, the jukebox playing, dancing, laughing, drinking, shrieking, mad. Sally was drunk, Emile was nuts, and Raymie was there too. Maybe an escaped lunatic stopped in off the highway, but why weren't Sally and Emile there? They lived there. Maybe they were murdered too and stuffed in the trunk of the murderer's car, on the way to Canada. But Emile was too big. Maybe the guy had a panel truck. So why hadn't he taken Mr. Asher too?

I didn't get any further because there was Asher's Bar and Grill sign, winking on and off, on and off. As though nothing had happened. It made me shiver, a thing I seldom do, thinking how full of beans I'd been a few hours ago coming back from town, seeing it wink on and off, on and off just like that. Thinking of absolutely nothing but putting off the evil moment of going home, and who might be there playing the jukebox, and who we could take for a couple of beers.

I'm telling you, either now or tomorrow, chums, you'd better stop and think it over. It could happen to you.

The yard was full of police cars and men, and even then at that hour of the morning, cars were stopping along the highway with people getting out to see what had happened.

Sergeant Fish Eye and Susan were waiting for us, and I was surprised to see that she was quite calm. At least, she *looked* calm on the outside, which was what she strived for at all times. How that girl hated to show a little garden-variety panic. Be reserved was her motto, even if dying of heartburn which asking for a Tums would cure.

"Well girls, it ain't pretty," Fish Eye said, leading the way through the gang around the door.

The grill was pretty crowded, photographers shooting pictures, men dusting powder on everything, and a lot of police standing around looking baffled. It wasn't hard, given those pusses. In fact, there was so much confusion that I almost missed Mr. Asher. He was still there all right, on the floor near the rickety booth. There was blood over the floor and spattered on the wall and over the table.

It was lucky George had me in a firm grip. Actually, after I saw that, he had to walk for both of us. All I could think was, Please God, don't have Susan look. Don't have her *look*. Because she would just quietly have died right there. But she never saw him. A photographer was standing on top of the bar taking flash pictures, and every time a bulb exploded, she jumped about a foot and walked a little faster. The sergeant could hardly keep up with her.

She had a way of getting sort of blind at crucial moments. Probably she noticed a cobweb on the mirror above the bar, or that one of the fingerprint men had a wart on his thumb, but the corpse she didn't see. Maybe there was some sort of self-preservation urge mixed up in her being that way. But even so, everything considered, I'm glad I'm not like that. What's the use of being preserved, if you don't know from what?

Anyhow, that's one for the birds, I mean psychiatrists. I should care less.

Lieutenant Feeley was holding court back in Sally's room, with a card table in front of him. It was so unlike the time I had seen him last that I almost laughed in his face. From being slightly hysterical. But then I felt Susan shiver and I calmed down. It's wonderful what you can do when you put your mind to it. I put mine to it for both of us.

Miriam Colwell

The room was strictly a shambles, and I've always wondered why he picked it, but the minds of big wheels are usually too simple for the average person to follow. They're looking for puzzles they can't understand. Half the bed covers were on the floor, and so was everything else that could be thrown, including broken glasses and a few smashed plates and ashtrays. But the closet door stood open and it was almost comical how neat it was inside. There were two clean uniforms, quite a few dresses, and some skirts and blouses hanging as trim as could be, with a shoe rack underneath full of shoes, and up on the shelf two hatboxes, one on top of the other, and a suit box with FILENE'S on it.

The lieutenant looked nervous in a very authoritative way. One of his eyes had a cast, and his hands were covered with black hair on the backs.

"You the two girls was in here last night?" he said, as though he was shooting puffed wheat out of a gun.

"We were here a while," I said.

"Well, give me your story. You first!" to Susan. "Just tell me what happened in your own words."

Susan had stumbled over part of a lamp as we came in, and she was still looking around in a dazed sort of way as though she was appalled at what a poor housekeeper Sally was. I nudged her and held on.

"Why, I . . . well, we . . ."

"Just go ahead in your own words," he shot out, as though any minute his joints might fly apart and this had to be attended to first.

"Well, we . . . we came in on our way home from the movies and . . . and had a glass of beer, and I . . . I met a friend who happened to be here, and we danced and ate a hot dog and then went on home."

"You both together all the time?"

"Why, why yes," she said, looking at me for reassurance. "We didn't *sit* together the whole time."

"Why not?"

"Well, Evelyn knew people I didn't and went to talk to them." She thought that was a silly question.

"But you would swear what your girlfriend was up to the whole evening? And she the same for you?"

"Why, of *course!*" she said, almost snickering in his face.

"Notice anything out of order during the time you were in here? Anyone seem peeved with the old man in your opinion?"

"No . . . ," she said, "everyone was having a good time, dancing and everything. It was . . . it was sort of a party. Except I noticed Mr. Asher talking to the waitress once or twice. I thought he was telling her to pay more attention to people, waiting on them. But she didn't get mad at him."

"All right," he said, shuffling papers around and looking as though he wanted to spit. "Now you."

"Well, in the first place, everyone was drinking quite a lot," I said, "including Mr. Asher and Emile and Sally, which wasn't unusual if you knew them. And they were all apt to get riled with each other. It *was* sort of a party like she said. Mr. Asher wanted us to stay and eat steak with him, but he went to sleep. Then Raymie came, Sally's boyfriend, and after a while they—he and Sally—came off down here—this is her room—and started making a racket, so Emile asked me to come back with him to see if we couldn't stop them fighting."

"Why *you*? Why was that?"

"Well, mainly because I was a girl," I said, giving him a timid smile, "and I knew Sally, and it was no good a man trying to reason with her. After she'd had a couple, she only had one thing on her mind where a man was concerned."

He grunted and gave me a sharp look, and then grinned for a small quarter of a second. "All right. So what happened?"

"They were having sort of an argument," I said, "and Sally threw a plate at Emile when we tried to stop them, so he got mad and threw some shoes at her, and I left, and we came home."

"You left them fighting?"

"I certainly did," I said. "It wasn't the sort of thing I wanted to be involved in. And when we left, Mr. Asher was sitting behind the cash register asleep."

"All right. Who was here while you girls were?"

I gave him the names I knew, and he slapped the card table a few times and said, "All right, girls, that's all for now, but stick around a while. I may want you again."

We drifted out and down the hall. George was there with his thumbs in his belt. He gave me a wink.

"Do you know who did it, Evelyn?" Sue whispered. The crazy kid expected me to know the answer to every question.

"Maybe I could guess," I muttered, so as not to disappoint her.

It was funny how turned upside-down and backwards everything was. Just an hour or so ago, the jukebox was banging and I was tearing around there, strictly the latest make. Riling old Sally, and needling Emile because he was such a blister, keeping Susie up when she was dead on her feet from acting like normal.

Now it was like looking into a crazy mirror and seeing the same thing. The same joint, full of fat cops and nervous detectives—and Mr. Asher would never drink another glass of lager.

Before I thought about it, there we were at the end of the hall watching all the commotion out in the grill. I took hold of Susan's hand, which was cold as ice.

"How long do we have to stay?" she asked, but she sounded all keyed up. "Wasn't it funny, the way he talked?"

Just then, a couple of men came in the door carrying a big basket thing. Everybody got out of the way to give them room, and bingo, they put Mr. Asher into it and that was that. I'd already heard of being taken out in a basket, and I guess I'll never forget the real McCoy. Even now it's not very pleasant to tell about.

Susan and I turned around like a pair of Siamese twins and winged back up the hall to the john, both of us as sick as cats. It was the one time in the world we reacted exactly alike.

I got there just in time and lost most of my insides in one minute flat. Susan held me up while it lasted, even washing my face with a Kleenex, and then while I was getting my breath back, she collapsed on the side of the tub and began to shake. It really scared me the way she shook, but all I could do was hold on and try to be calm. Talk about the halt supporting the blind. It would have been better if she could have been sick too, but it's the lot of some people to always pick the hard way.

After a while, she got back under control a little and said, "C-c-could I have a g-g-glass of water?"

There wasn't a glass in that crummy bathroom, so I said, "I'll go get one. You wait right here."

We were certainly a keen-looking pair. You could have drawn us simultaneously through a knothole with room to spare. For a minute I dreaded showing myself with all those palookas standing around, but then thinking what a lousy, dirty deal it was for a poor old guy who'd always been pretty swell to me, I didn't care. The hell with them. I shut the door on Susan and started for the kitchen. My legs felt a little uncertain as to whether they would tag along or not.

"Got to get Sue a glass of water," I said to George. "She don't feel so hot."

There I was wavering down the hall on my straw legs with a couple of cops staring at me, and all of a sudden I thought of the peanut-butter jar. The minute it came into my head I knew what I was going to do. As though I had been thinking it out for a month. Sometimes it really scares me to find plans all made in my mind without my even knowing it.

I pulled the kitchen door halfway shut behind me, without seeming to, and then there wasn't time to be cautious or hash the situation over. The other door behind the bar was partly closed, and anyway, you couldn't see back into the corner from there.

There never was a clearer case of He Who Hesitates Is Lost, one of my favorite mottoes, so I grabbed a chair, jumped up on it, and managed to reach that jar behind the waxed paper from sheer necessity.

The perspiration was running off me like rain, and my knees wobbled so I could hardly get down. But I did, and shoved the old chair away into the corner. When I tried to unscrew the top, my hands were shaking like Grandpa's used to, but you couldn't have stopped me then.

I fished the roll out with my right hand and got it poked down inside my sneaker under my instep while at the same time with my left, I pushed that jar and the moldy bologna way down into the garbage can under a week's mess, and got the top back on the damn can too. About one second later I was getting a glass down out of the cupboard when Lieutenant Feeley came prancing in.

"Your friend's sick, is she?" he said, but one look at me seemed to convince him. "You look pretty white-livered yourself. Better go sit in your car. If I need you I'll send a man out."

"She wanted some water," I said. "I had to get a glass."

"All right, all right," he said. "For God's sake, go out and get some air. I got enough troubles without you on my hands too."

"Can't we go home now?"

"Hold your horses, hold your horses. We're bringing the others in. I want you two around while I get their stories. And keep clear of those damned reporters. Tell them you can't talk yet."

Oh brother. Reporters. Our names in the paper, mixed up in a messy deal like this. I could see Mrs. Becker's face and it made me sick all over again. Because naturally Susan's being there was seventy percent my fault.

"Oh golly, Lieutenant," I said, "honest, this is awful on a girl like Susan. I mean, she's sensitive and like that. And her aunt might really have a heart attack. Couldn't you just let us sneak out of here right now? Golly, I feel responsible to her folks." I gave him all the ammunition I could muster in my weakened condition. Which he ignored. It made me sore. What did he have to lose by being human? Of course, I was too upset to be thinking very straight.

"My God," I said, "we've told you all there is to tell. All the names and everything. What do you want, our gizzards?"

"Hold on, miss, take it easy. I'm calling the shots here, and I say stick around! See! Get that straight. If your friend's so delicate, she shouldn't be playing around a dive like this in the first place.

You were both looking for trouble when you came in here and now you got it."

"Lieutenant Feeley," I said, very softly and sweetly, feeling that big old lump under my instep, "you know there's others I've known of to be in places they wouldn't want advertised. Especially when they got somebody else's wife along."

He shot me a full barrel of bird shot, growling something unintelligible. But his ammunition bounced right off. I knew what I knew. And after a minute or two of looking me over, during which I held onto my go-ahead-and-call-me-if-you-dare-to expression, never batting an eyelash, he knew I knew.

Last fall, Charlie and I were coming home from roller-skating one night, very late, as the rink was forty-five miles from home and we skated until twelve, and a few miles above Asher's, Charlie had to get out and investigate the underbrush. Which he did about every five miles after one glass of beer.

It wasn't dark, though there wasn't a moon as it was cloudy. He came snickering back to the car, saying some cop was parked way back in the old wood road. He could hear the shortwave radio going way back in there.

"Want to go take a peek?" he said.

"My God, you're nosy."

"Yeh, and you're worse," he yakked. So we went sneaking back into the woods, feeling really above ourselves. It wasn't that we cared who it was or anything—just that it was such a wacky thing to do, sneak up on a cop.

We couldn't see much, except that it was a car with a shortwave aerial sticking up on every corner, but Charlie kept inching up a little closer and a little closer, pulling me along with him. He had times when he was a real wild child. We could hear the speaker sputtering static and numbers and so forth. Then all at once, it got quite plain and said, "Lieutenant Feeley, calling Lieutenant Feeley."

There was a lot of scrambling around in the backseat, and in a minute he put on the overhead light. Brother! That certainly taught me a lesson. When you're up to mischief, always remember there *might* be someone on the outside looking in. I'll omit who he was with, other than it was a great big surprise.

We backtracked out of that locality, but fast. Charlie kept having such fits all the rest of the way home that I had to drive.

Lieutenant Feeley finally dragged out his cigarettes and offered me one. Old Golds. But I took it anyway. He was so quiet I thought, This time, sister, you've really cooked your little goosey. My legs got weaker and weaker, expecting handcuffs any minute, trying to bribe a cop and being loaded with stolen goods into the bargain, but I managed to look him right in the eye, not giving an inch. Except that I concentrated on the eye with the cast in it.

Then he reached over and gave me a pat on the shoulder. I almost died with relief.

"Okay, Evelyn," he said, "that's your name, isn't it? Now listen, it's going to be busy as hell around here and I'm going to send you kids home. This is no place for youngsters. If you should think of anything I ought to know, come tell me anytime; otherwise, neither of you'll be bothered."

"Do our names have to be in the paper?"

"There's no need of your names being dragged in that I can see," he said, wiping his forehead. "All right, now. We agreed? That decent enough?"

"That's very decent, Lieutenant," I said, with dignity. "Thank you from the bottom of my heart."

"All right, all right," he said with a little twitch of a grin. "Now get the hell out of here, quick."

It was daylight outside. George went to the car with us and shooed everyone off that was hanging around wanting to ask questions. Then we were actually heading home. Neither Francis nor I felt up to going very fast. Susan sat like a block of stone, staring straight ahead.

"You feel better, honey?"

"I . . . I guess so."

We gave each other a sort of wavery smile.

The sky began to get all red. I kept gulping in that lovely-tasting morning air as though I'd never get enough. It was really beautiful. The lake was like glass, not a ripple, and the trees and everything looked clean and unpolluted and washed with dew.

I can appreciate it more now thinking about it than I did then.

That lump under my instep seemed to get bigger and bigger the farther away we got. How I ever walked out of that kitchen without limping right in front of him is a miracle.

Don't think I had any qualms over taking it. I didn't. Why should I leave it there for the police to find? Besides, it might have belonged to Mr. Asher himself. He had funny ways of doing things sometimes. Maybe whoever it was, they had forgotten all about it. That bologna had certainly been there a long time.

The sun was coming up out of the ocean as we drove down the hill into town. The harbor water was tinted pink, and there wasn't a sign of life anywhere, except out on the bay, three or four boats moving around, looking very white and graceful.

When we stopped in front of her house, Susan didn't move. "If I just didn't have to go in," she said. She sounded desperate and dead at the same time. "If I just didn't have to *talk* about it anymore, or think about it . . ."

"I'm coming with you," I said. "It's all my fault, Sue; you know that, don't you?"

"No. It isn't your fault," she said. "No, don't *say* that."

We managed to smile at each other, and believe me, we were two ghosts not even mothers could love, stringy hair, pale as onions, and Sue's eyes looked like two holes burned in a blanket.

"Okay," I said. "I'm too tired to argue, old girl." Right then, we were real friends in every sense of the word. It was a sort of feeling you don't ever lose, even if you change and the other person changes, and you meet ten years later and don't know each other anymore except to be false-face cordial and say, "Remember when we this and that . . . Oh my God, what crazy kids we were in those days. . . ." And so on, having nothing whatever to talk about anymore.

But this feeling is a sort of thing in itself that you can take out once in a while and polish off and feel sad about and good about at the same time, over your whole life. Sue and I had it, and that was a day we really knew it. In spite of being Chinese puzzles to each other most of the rest of the time.

Mrs. Becker opened the door before we ever got to it. She was dressed, with her hair wound in braids around her head, not combed in a pug as she wore it when she really got up.

"Thank you for bringing Susan home, Evelyn," she said, "but you'd better go right along now."

Susan stopped dead. She looked as though someone had knocked her out but she couldn't fall down.

These were my walking papers. Mrs. Becker and I understood each other, you could say that. Of course, from my viewpoint, she could have waited, because I was feeling like a pretty sad-sack just then, but I guess from hers she had waited too long. The way she saw it, I might have put a blight on Susan forever. I didn't think so, but we were both entitled to our own opinions. Anyway, there wasn't going to be any more jelly tarts in Sue's lunch for Evelyn, or any more days together at the movies.

Well, that twenty-four hours saw a lot of things laid to rest, Mr. Asher not least of all, bless his soul.

"Sure, Mrs. Becker," I said. "I know what you mean. I just wanted to tell you they won't bother Sue anymore, for questions or anything. And her name won't be in the paper, either."

It didn't make any dent at all. Maybe she just didn't believe it.

"Come, Susan," she said, and I might as well have been a tree standing there.

Sue was trying her darndest not to cry. Her lips were quivering so she couldn't talk back, but anyway, it was a lost cause. She gave a little moan and turned and hugged me as hard as she could, tears just pouring down her cheeks, all the ones she'd held back. I guess I may have been crying a little too. We were both of us so tired we were tottering.

"Oh gosh, don't, Sue," I whispered, "don't cry. It's okay. Honest, I don't care. Everything'll be all right."

Mrs. Becker started to pull her away, not hard, because she wasn't too happy about the whole thing herself.

"See you down on the shore, same place," I whispered.

If this was the end of something pretty important, I figured Mrs. Becker owed us a chance for a decent good-bye. Of course I know now there's no such thing. How could there be, if you really care about what you're leaving? It's murder.

So I blew my nose and Francis and I went home.

Thank God my mother wasn't up yet. I just managed to get upstairs when I heard her stirring.

The funniest thing was, I didn't even count the money. Somehow or other it didn't make much difference right then. I pushed it way into the toe of my sneaker and threw the sneaker under the bureau. Then I fell in bed.

The next thing I knew after that, it was twelve o'clock, and the noon whistle on the firehouse woke me up. Also the sun was in my eyes. For a while I just lay there. I couldn't seem to move. My brain felt the same way, as though someone had hauled off and given it a wallop.

But it was a new day. And finally life began to stir. When I was actually on my feet and there were no broken bones showing, my head commenced functioning too. In a small way.

The sun was shining, and the town was really going to be on its ear. A murder was the most flabbergasting event that had ever happened around here.

But I couldn't quite take it in. No, that wasn't it. It was in too far. I couldn't seem to pull it out in the light where it would be something to feel excited and hepped up about. It was lodged in my insides too close. And there was nothing pleasant or exciting about it, believe me. It was too damned actual. If I could have erased that whole twenty-four hours, I would have been a happy girl.

But there was no point in mooning around forever. So my first move was to crawl under the bureau and fish out my sneaker. There was eighty-five dollars in that roll! Plus a five-dollar bill in my jacket pocket and some change. I sat down on the bed and just looked at it, but even seeing the bills didn't make much difference. My brain wasn't in a digesting mood.

Finally I stowed it away in a safe place, except the sixty-three cents change, and went downstairs.

"Morning, Marm," I said, giving her a peck on the back of the neck. One thing did seep through then, how surprised she was going to be to see her forty-two bucks.

"I should say as much," she snapped, turning around as though I had bitten her. "What have you got to say for yourself, lady? Running off and leaving me just about wild with those orders."

My mother often sounded much crosser than she really was; that is, than she was if you gave her time to cool off, which I was always glad to do. And everything had been taken care of after a fashion. Old lady Ogden had her oatmeal bread for breakfast. There wasn't much left to fret about, unless you wanted to dwell on bygones.

Somehow, just watching her slat around the kitchen, picking up yesterday's paper, sounding so normal, brought me ninety percent back to life.

"You hear what happened up at Asher's Bar and Grill last night, Marm?"

"I haven't been out of the house, and no one's been since your father left. How would I be apt to know?"

"Well, Mr. Asher was murdered, that's all. Right in his own beer parlor."

She sat down with a plump and stared at me. Everything else went right out of her head, naturally.

I got a doughnut out of the breadbox and poured myself a cup of coffee.

"Who in the world would do a thing like that around here?"

"That's what the police want to know, I guess."

"I'm glad I didn't know it with you out running the roads last night," she said, fanning herself with her apron. "I should have gone straight out of my mind with worry."

"I'm going downtown for a paper, Ma. Maybe they'll have it in already."

She sat there rocking back and forth, flapping her apron and not even asking questions.

"Give me a cup of coffee, dear. My soul, what will happen next? A murder! Right *here*. It just don't seem possible."

When I slammed the screen door, she called out, "Now be careful, Evelyn. Don't you go near there unless your father goes with you. It isn't safe with maniacs running loose."

Though I hadn't thought of it beforehand, Francis went straight down the Lighthouse Road and stopped by the boathouse. Just like yesterday. But brother, speaking of water over the dam. The mushrooms were still there, growing as bright as buttons in the nice cool shade. That path always had a special smell, from the trees or something. I kicked off the heads of a few of the real orangey mushrooms so they would be keeping up with the rest of the world, where there'd been some changes made.

It was comical when I got out in sight of the rocks, with the sea growling away on the ledges down at low-tide mark. There sat Susan as though she'd been there since yesterday, and sure enough, old Double Trouble was right there too, both of them staring out at the bay, with the breeze ruffling Susie's hair. His probably had so much lotion plastered on the curls a hurricane wouldn't have disturbed it.

Susie looked pretty wan, as though she hadn't slept much.

"Hi honey," I said. "Hello, Hine. What is this, a re-take?"

He didn't smile, naturally, though God knows it doesn't take much effort. Just a little twitch and there you are.

"Hello, Evelyn."

"I was afraid you weren't coming," Susan said, and then sort of bit her lip. She kept picking up little pieces of granite and pounding the ledge with them, not looking up.

"Anyone hear anything this morning?" I inquired, to keep this lively repartee on its feet. "I just crawled out."

"From whose knothole?" Hine said, but with no real spark, just from habit. "Who's got a fag?"

I didn't, but believe me, I would have swallowed a carton whole before this wise guy got to clog his lungs with one from me.

"The finger's pointing at the cook," he said, giving me his Bogart black look, No. 2. "They've rounded up everyone else. The lieutenant's sent out a twelve-state alarm."

"They're bound to find him," I said, "even if they're looking. He's too big to hide."

All at once Susan said, "I've got to go. I *had* to wait till you came."

From her voice I knew she wasn't kidding. "Why, Susie?"

"Mrs. . . . Mrs. Ogden's going to drive me down to Odessa's. I'm . . . going to be there all summer. Maybe longer than that. She's probably waiting with Aunt Clara now, but . . . but I had to say good-bye."

She still couldn't move, just sat there crumbling rock between her fingers.

But Hine went off like a firecracker. "That bunch of snobs, for Christ's sake? Why didn't you say so? They'll ruin every chance you ever had."

"You're a big help," I said, "and furthermore, it's none of your God-damn business. Come on, Susie, I'll walk out the path with you."

I don't think she ever could have gotten up, otherwise. "'Bye, Hine." She managed to smile at him, and then practically ran.

We didn't say a word all the way through the woods out to the boathouse, not needing to. Her hand was as cold as ice. When we got to Francis, I stopped and said, "Susie, dear, have fun. I'll . . . I'll miss you like hell. You know that."

She didn't answer or even look at me, just pulled my hand against her cheek for a minute.

I could feel the wetness, and then she went off up the road, stumbling as though she couldn't see.

So that was that. Luckily I found an old Kleenex to blow my nose on, which I had done more of, God knows, in the last few hours than practically a lifetime.

After a minute or two, I could see that maybe this was the best thing that ever happened to Susan, and if so, I had some of the credit, though my bit was contributed sort of hindside and backwards. Living with Odessa and the boy-genius she could really get a load of, well, whatever it was they had, about which I was no authority. But maybe for Susan it would be just the right charge. Anyhow, one big item, it got her out of this burg and into greener pastures.

I sat down on Francis's running board. The sun was hot. Someone was scraping a boat down on the rocks below the boathouse.

Just sitting there, I felt a sort of empty calm, not really sad, not really anything, with the heat on my head, watching a couple of kids rowing around in circles across the cove, and suddenly a revelation came to me. As clear as anything in the world.

Francis and I were leaving too! Today. Now. What was there to hold us back? Forty-two dollars to my mother, that left me forty-eight. My mother would feel bad naturally, but she knew I wasn't cut out to hang around here. She could get any number of kids to deliver the cakes. On time, too. They would be more scared of her than I was.

Hine came loping out of the path, looking as though he wished someone would cut his throat to give him a real excuse to be nasty.

"Well?" he said.

"She's gone."

"Yeh, very touching scene. Christ, I could have done a lot for that kid."

"Oh my God," I said, "you're not the only can opener in the world."

"You're pretty complicated, aren't you, Evelyn?" he said. You never knew whether he was being sarcastic or not. One time so, next time, not so.

"You want a lift? I'm in sort of a hurry too."

"You, too? Where in hell are you going?"

"Marblehead," I said. "I got a girlfriend down there in a hotel who's going to get me a job."

It was a great relief to know where I was going. Iris would get me a job all right, she'd be tickled pink to see me. She was really pretty big-hearted if not terribly bright. I couldn't wait to get started now that it was all settled.

"For the love of God," Hine said. "What's the score around here, anyhow? You're going down to *Marblehead*? In the jalopy?"

"I certainly am. Kindly don't refer to Francis as a jalopy. He's not deaf."

He began to laugh, which made him quite attractive in a weird sort of way.

"How about giving me a ride down?" he said. "I don't want to be marooned up here on this desert island. I'll keep you company down to Boston. You'd never find the way alone, anyhow."

"Sure," I said, "if you want to pay for half the gas."

About the Author
Miriam Colwell

If ever a writer could write authentically about what it was like to grow up, live, and work in a Maine coastal village, appreciate its heritage and recognize the changes brought by time, it would be Miriam Colwell. As postmaster for more than thirty years in Prospect Harbor—the Down East town where she was born and raised and that her ancestors helped settle—she watched the daily comings and goings of townsfolk and visitors, and was witness to the events, issues and emotions that shaped their lives. Her observations, combined with what Maine author Sanford Phippen calls Colwell's "authentic Down East voice and dry, subtle sense of humor," shaped her four novels and forged them into a testament of coastal life and change in the 1940s and 1950s.

Courtesy of Miriam Colwell

Miriam Colwell, 1950s

Her voice, however, was not fashioned solely in Maine. She spent a few years amongst the literary and fine arts crowd of New York City and then brought a bit of that world home to Prospect Harbor. The mixture of those perspectives and her innate writing talent helped create a voice that captured the time and still resonates in many ways today.

"Everyone who wants to get acquainted with the whole body of Maine literature in the twentieth century should read Miriam Colwell," wrote Betsy Graves in *The Puckerbrush Review*. "She

Miriam Colwell, 2007
photo by Linda Eastman

represents an important piece in the body, an authentic voice of Maine."

Miriam Colwell was born in 1917 in Prospect Harbor. She has lived there most of her life, save for a year at college and her time in New York City. In the later '70s through the 1980s she lived in Georgia for six months of the year. Today, she lives in the lovely large farmhouse where she was born, a house built by her great-great-great-grandfather in 1817.

In the late eighteenth century, Colwell's mother's family, the Coles, moved from Massachusetts to help settle the town, building a sawmill in Prospect Harbor on the Schoodic Peninsula. Her father's family also made their way Down East, coming from Nova Scotia and settling first on Petit Manan Point before moving to the village as well. Her grandfather, George Colwell, was a pioneer in the growth of the lobster industry.

When Miriam Colwell was but two years old, her mother, Genevieve, died in the Spanish influenza epidemic that swept the nation. The epidemic had already claimed the life of Colwell's only sister. Meanwhile, her father, Clarence, suffered from tuberculosis and was forced to live in near seclusion with his parents, leaving Miriam's maternal grandparents to raise her. She saw her father often, though, visiting him when his health permitted at her paternal grandparents' home on the other side of the village. Despite the loss of her mother and her father's illness, Colwell recalls her childhood fondly. Both sides of her family provided a "very warm, supportive childhood. There is no question . . . I was so spoiled, I was never asked to do anything or taught to do any cooking or cleaning or bed making or dishwashing or anything. I never was expected to do anything except play," she said in a 2005 interview for the Smithsonian *Archives of American Art*.

Grandfather Louis Ponvert Cole ran a general store and served as the village postmaster as his ancestors did. Grandmother Susan Blance Cole served meals during the summer for a few regular patrons, perhaps as much for the social benefits as for the added income. Her grandmother also surrounded herself with books, which Miriam Colwell, a reader from childhood, appreciated greatly.

Colwell attended a one-room schoolhouse in Prospect Harbor until she was old enough for high school, where—although shy and quite "an innocent"—she won prizes in public speaking contests and began to write poetry. She graduated from Winter Harbor High School in 1935 as class valedictorian and, using some money left to her by her mother, she headed for the University of Maine in Orono. However, after only a year at the university, she decided it was not for her. She returned home and went to work at her grandfather's store.

Meanwhile, her poetry would soon garner attention from some important corners. Sometime after returning home from Orono, Colwell received an invitation from her high school friend, Louise Young, to come to Corea to meet some of her new acquaintances. Young's mother had opened a small summer eatery, Katie's Restaurant, which very quickly became popular with all the summer visitors. Young, as an ebullient seventeen-year-old waitress, became equally popular. During Colwell's visit, which was to change her life, Young introduced her to two New York City schoolteachers and to Chenoweth Hall, with whom Colwell would eventually share her life and travels.

"They were completely exotic to me and I was exotic to them ... They treated me as this exotic object, this tall, blonde Maine Down East girl who was writing poetry, a budding Millay," she told her 2005 interviewer. She blossomed under the admiration.

Hall, who came to be renowned for her music, paintings, sculpture, and writing, was then working at a New York City advertising agency. Though very different in some ways, Hall and Colwell struck up an immediate friendship, and soon Colwell was driving down to the city for visits, eventually moving there in the late 1930s. The two women shared an apartment in Manhattan, a long way from Prospect Harbor. Colwell passed her time exploring the city, writing freelance advertising copy, peddling an exercise gizmo called Trimtummy, conducting market research surveys, and, most importantly, enjoying the artistic milieu of Hall and her circle of friends. Soon, Colwell established herself as part of that circle.

However, after two years in the city, Colwell learned that Grandfather Cole had reached the mandatory postmaster retirement age of seventy. The job always had been held by someone in the family, and her grandmother was anxious for Colwell to return home to be near her family. Colwell reluctantly agreed, and Hall was ready to relocate with her. And so at age twenty-three, Colwell left New York City and returned to Prospect Harbor where she became the youngest postmaster in the country. Fortunately, it was a relatively easy job that gave her time to pursue other interests—and to begin writing. With a growing network of friends, writers and artists, life in Prospect Harbor was from the beginning a blend of two worlds. Marsden Hartley, Berenice Abbott, Ruth Moore, Katharine Butler Hathaway, and John Marin were among the well-known writers and artists of the time that Colwell and Hall (who passed away in 1999) entertained in Prospect Harbor. They also traveled extensively, both in the U.S. and abroad.

Yet, when Colwell began writing her novels, she wrote not about the "exotic" life of which she had become a part, but rather drew inspiration from her Maine heritage and the lives of all the people she knew growing up and with whom she still spoke every day as she handed out their mail. Her first effort was *Wind off the Water,* published by Random House in 1945. The book tells the story of three brothers in a Maine fishing village, two content and one decidedly not.

"*Wind off the Water* was an attempt to portray the life of a small rural fishing community," she said. "In one's early twenties there seems to be the confidence that your particular insight may be illuminating enough to warrant exposure."

Critics offered their praise.

"Its distinction lies in its firm sense of the seasons and the life of the village, and in its authentic Yankee talk. It cuts deep. Miss Colwell is a youngster to watch," said *The Providence Journal*.

Colwell quickly followed *Wind* in 1947 with *Day of the Trumpet*, a fictional tale loosely based on her grandfather's experience in the fledgling Maine lobster industry. Eight years later, and after a few years working on another novel that went unpublished "for good reason," she wrote *Young*, the story of a day in the life of two small-town Maine girls who have just graduated from high school. Colwell said this was the most enjoyable book to write and the only one that was in any way autobiographical.

Once again, critics praised Colwell. Robert Linder said *Young* was "[an] amazingly perceptive study of the modern girl in her late adolescence. What J. D. Salinger did for the [American] male, Miriam Colwell has done for the [American] female."

And finally during the 1950s, she wrote *Contentment Cove* (which she originally titled *Plus and Minus*). However, the book went unpublished and she filed it in the chicken house behind her home. After about fifteen years of writing, with three published novels and two unpublished, she stopped writing for reasons unclear to her even today. "Perhaps feeling I had said what I had to say, perhaps because life was too engaging," she said recently. She moved on to other pursuits.

But she would be published again. Some fifty years later, while sorting through the contents of the chicken house file, she came across her forgotten manuscript. She reread it and enjoyed every word. This time it found a publisher and was released by Puckerbrush Press in 2006.

Contentment Cove is set in a picturesque Down East village of the same name during the 1950s. The story takes place over a matter of days one summer, and is told from the illuminating perspectives of three women—a local shopkeeper, an artist, and a wealthy retiree—whose lives become entwined, pleasantly at first and then tragically. The novel is "a gently satirical treatment of summer people and natives . . . We are dealing with the same things now as in the '50s and '60s," Colwell said in the 2005 Smithsonian interview. With *Contentment Cove* as with each of her novels, she said, "I was trying to present a true look at the world around me."

Says Phippen: "The novel was way before its time with its depiction of well-to-do newcomers who pick a small Maine village for their year-round living, only to become terribly disenchanted with the place. Colwell, with her wit and sharp, cold eye, does a very nice job revealing *Contentment Cove*."

Colwell believes that within the fifteen-year span of time during which *Wind off the Water*, *Young*, and *Contentment Cove* are set, the changing coast is clearly reflected. *Wind off the Water* is about an isolated community dependent on lobster fishing and the sardine industry. There are no summer people mentioned. In *Young*, one of the characters spends some time working for a summer visitor, and a few other summer folks are mentioned. By the time of *Contentment Cove,* the "folks from away" are having a greater impact and the conflicts are building.

"In their own small way," Colwell said, "I think these three books bear witness to and portray the changing demographics and changing culture that has taken place along coastal areas over the last fifty years."

And Colwell, who has closely watched that change for nearly ninety years, should know as well as anyone.